WA

WASP Sting

Lee A. Sweetapple

This is a work of fiction. All characters, names, incidents, organizations, and dialogue in this novel are either the product of the author's imagination or are used fictitiously.

ISBN-13: 9780692772898
ISBN-10: 0692772898
Library of Congress Control Number: 2016914939
Eclectic Manor Publishing, Marshall, VA

This book is dedicated to the Women Airforce Service Pilots (WASP) and all the stories that they can't tell.

Acknowledgments

To WASP pilot Shirley Slade and Eagle Squadron Ace Gregory Augustus "Gus" Daymond, who strangely look like younger versions of my wife and me in their photos from World War II.

To Martin Bowman and his fantastic book *P-51 Mustang Combat Missions*.

To the Collings Foundation for providing me with the experience of a lifetime flying their P-51C, *Betty Jane*.

To my wife, Lyn, for buying me the ride of a lifetime on my fiftieth birthday.

To the Commemorative Air Force for preserving beautiful flying museums.

To the Commemorative Air Force Red Tail Squadron's educational-outreach program for bringing encouragement and guidance to children of every race and creed.

To Lyn "MOD" Sweetapple, Colonel Otto "Ottomatic" Busher, and Domingo "Redleg" Chang for editing and technical advice.

CHAPTER 1

Mines Field, Los Angeles, 06 0945 January 1944

Trudy Andrich looked at the instrument panel once more before she released the brakes and let the rumbling Rolls-Royce Merlin engine slowly pull the P-51D Mustang away from the parking area. With the tail of the airplane resting on a small wheel, the front of the fuselage and the blur of the propeller seemed to tower above Trudy's head and blocked her vision directly in front of the aircraft. Trudy glanced between the right and left sides of the Mustang, and following procedure, she kept the stick in a neutral position to allow the tail wheel to pivot. This procedure permitted Trudy to see where she was going by using a series of S-turns to weave her way down the taxiway to the run-up area. Strapped into the Mustang, Trudy felt like she was in a saddle, riding some gigantic and powerful beast. The main landing gear under the wings provided audible and tactile feedback as they crossed the joints in the concrete taxiway and gave the sensation of a trotting race horse moving on four legs instead of three wheels. The engine ran at near idle during the short trip to the run-up area.

Trudy pulled into the run-up area, set the brakes, and began her final checks before takeoff. It was a cool Southern California morning. There was still a layer of fog over the ocean just a few miles away, but the sky was clear, and the sun was turning the cockpit of the Mustang into a greenhouse. The heat from the engine was already making its way into the cockpit, and Trudy's feet were beginning to feel the heat. Trudy noticed the beads of sweat on her forehead, and she was anxious to get off the ground and into the refreshingly cool air up above.

Trudy pressed hard on both rudder pedals, keeping the brakes firmly set as she moved the throttle forward until the manifold pressure read no more than thirty; otherwise, the powerful engine would cause the Mustang to nose over. All the while, Trudy kept her eyes on the instrument panel to check the magnetos and watch for other anomalies on the gauges that revealed the health of the engine. The twelve-cylinder engine roared and tugged hard against the brakes. The torque of the engine twisted the plane and made the left wing dip slightly. Twice, the engine seemed to lose rhythm as it missed but returned to normal rhythm. Trudy heard the change and kept the throttle forward for a few more seconds than normal to make sure that the interruption in rhythm was just a fluke, maybe due to moisture. She remembered the thick fog that blanketed Mines Field during the night just a few hours ago.

Satisfied that all was normal, Trudy taxied forward to the runway and contacted the tower: "Mines Tower, Mustang Two Seven Mike Oscar, ready for takeoff."

"Mustang Two Seven Mike Oscar, you are cleared for takeoff. Make right traffic. You get feet wet today and the scenic view. Contact Palm Springs when in sight."

"Mustang Two Seven Mike Oscar cleared for takeoff with right traffic," Trudy repeated back to the tower and turned onto the runway continuing her roll forward as she lined up with the stripes on the runway and moved the throttle slowly forward.

Trudy compensated for the more than fourteen-hundred-horsepower Rolls-Royce engine's torque with rudder pedal and slight back pressure on the stick to keep the tail wheel in contact with the runway until there was enough air going over the control surfaces to allow her to correct with rudder and ailerons alone. She needed to keep the plane in the middle of the runway with the tail down until she saw the airspeed indicator reach seventy miles per hour. With the tail up, she now had a clear view of the end of the runway. At 120 mph, Trudy eased back on the stick, and the Mustang leaped into the air. Trudy retracted the gear before she cleared the end of the runway and felt the airplane surge forward still gaining airspeed. Trudy retracted her flaps just before she started her right turn away from the field; she flipped the fuel-boost switch from emergency to normal as she went "feet wet" over the ocean, still climbing to her cruising altitude before starting her turn toward Palm Springs Field, where the six Browning .50-caliber machine guns would be placed in the wings. After refueling, the Mustang would begin its hopscotch path across the country and eventually be ferried across the ocean to England to enter the war.

As a member of the Women Airforce Service Pilots (WASP), Trudy Andrich flew as a test pilot and ferry pilot working out of the North American company's Southern California aircraft plant adjacent to Mines Field, just outside of Los Angeles. America's newest and hottest fighter, the P-51D Mustang, was made there, and Trudy was fulfilling a lifelong dream to fly the fastest airplanes made, even though women pilots were prohibited from serving in the Army Air Corps as pilots. It frustrated Trudy that she could not fly this plane into combat, knowing that she was a better pilot with far more hours under her belt than most of the green young pilots sent to combat in Europe in these planes. Trudy completed her turn west and thought about what it would be like to fly this bird in combat, escorting B-17 bombers deep into Germany. Her daydream was interrupted as the Rolls-Royce Merlin engine missed repeatedly, and the plane shuddered with each missed cylinder. Trudy watched the rpms drop as she adjusted the throttle to provide more fuel and quickly adjusted the boost control as the engine sputtered to a stop.

"Mayday, Mayday, Mines Tower. This is Mustang Two Seven Mike Oscar; I have lost power and am returning to the field."

Lieutenant Busher jumped to his feet in the control tower. He leaned forward, close to the slanted window, and peered westward trying to see the aircraft in distress. "Mustang Two Seven Mike Oscar, you are cleared for landing. I will alert emergency services."

Lieutenant Busher switched to the base intercom. "Attention on the field: aircraft inbound for an emergency landing."

At the airport fire station, more than a dozen firemen jumped into their gear and scrambled into their trucks, memories still strong of the crash landing at the field just two weeks before when the Army Air Corps test pilot did not survive the crash.

Inside the Mines Field headquarters building, a young sergeant burst into the conference room where the base commander Colonel Buck

Straight was meeting with Major Roderick "Rod" Jackson. "Sir, I'm sorry to interrupt, but we have a Mustang inbound with engine failure landing dead stick."

Colonel Straight turned to Major Jackson. "Come with me, Major." Looking back at the sergeant, he said, "Sergeant, get me some binoculars ASAP, and call for my jeep. I'll be outside."

Colonel Straight ushered the major to the front of the building as the young sergeant ran to the phone at his desk across from the conference-room door.

On board the Mustang, Trudy pointed the nose toward Mines Field and put the aircraft into a flat glide, keeping the airspeed just under 115 mph since the plane was heavy with fuel. Trudy tried to restart the engine and felt the sudden buffet that warned her that she was close to stall speed, so she pushed the stick a little bit farther forward and checked her airspeed again. A full stall would be disastrous. She tried to restart the engine several more times and soon judged that the distraction was too great, and the cause seemed futile.

"Concentrate on a dead-stick landing," Trudy said out loud as she attempted to steer toward the end of the runway.

Instinctively she reached for the flaps and gear switches but remembered her instructor yelling at her class emphatically: "If you lose power and need to attempt a dead-stick landing, keep the flaps and gear up!"

Trudy saw the end of the runway approaching fast. From the tower, Lieutenant Busher crackled loudly through her earphones: "Trudy, we have fire engines standing by. Crack open your canopy so it doesn't jam shut when you land."

"Thanks, Lieutenant, I'm on it. Wish me luck." Trudy wasn't very religious, but, having been brought up in a devout Russian Orthodox Ukrainian home, she crossed herself left-handed, keeping her right hand on the stick as she crossed the threshold of the runway. The plane floated for a moment, delaying impact for an extra two seconds as the wings went into ground effect. The slowly spinning propeller in front of her stopped as two of the four blades struck the runway, just before Trudy felt the impact and the sudden deceleration. A horrible scrapping sound, the smell of oil first, and then aviation gas as flames shot up in front of her, and the plane spun like a top before it came to rest at the edge of the runway. Trudy unstrapped herself and struggled with the canopy as she rolled out of the plane, onto the wing and then slid off the wing onto the hard concrete. The fire had already spread to the grass next to the runway on the other side of the plane, but the left wing remained intact and Trudy noted with relief the lack of fuel on the runway. She rolled onto her hands and knees and sprang to her feet, sprinting fifty yards away from her Mustang before turning around to see it now fully engulfed in fire as fuel continued to spill out of the fractured right wing into the grass.

The first fire truck screamed past her on the runway, almost hitting her. As she watched it pass and almost flipped the driver an obscene gesture, she heard screeching tires and turned as a jeep skidded to a stop not more than ten feet away from her. Colonel Straight jumped out of the front passenger seat and ran up to Trudy. "Are you all right?" The colonel yelled above the sirens and the roar of the flames as he looked her up and down.

"I'm fine, Colonel. The engine stopped, same as two weeks ago for Marty."

"You're bleeding." Colonel Straight said pointing at Trudy's knees.

Trudy looked down and saw the shredded and bloody fabric over her knees, and as she reached down, she realized that the skin was also missing from the palms of both hands. As the adrenaline started to wear off, Trudy felt the sting of road rash on both hands, elbows, and knees. Memories of the results of riding her bike down the steepest hill in town when she was barely ten distracted her for a moment.

Jackson jumped somewhat awkwardly off the jeep from the back seat and joined the colonel, looking gobsmacked as he stared at the beautiful blond pilot who had just survived the total destruction of her aircraft. "You're a dame!" he blurted out, still staring at her.

Colonel Straight cracked a wry smile. "She is a pilot. And after this landing, I'd say she is the best pilot I have ever met. Well done, Trudy." Colonel Straight held out his hand to shake.

Trudy started to instinctively grab the colonel's hand, and noticing the blood from her missing palm running down her arm, she instead held up her hand to show the colonel.

"Major Rod Jackson, at your service. Are you all right?" Rod said as he ran over to Trudy.

"I'm OK, I think. I'm Trudy Andrich. Nice to meet you."

"Beautiful and rich, but I'll bet that you have heard that before."

"At least once, in the last week alone. You fighter pilots must share your lines."

Colonel Straight stepped forward and put an arm around Trudy like a dad comforting a young daughter and helped Trudy into the front seat of the jeep. "Let's get you to the hospital. We don't need to supervise the firemen. This is the most fun they have had in a long time. Get in the jeep, Major." The colonel ordered Major Jackson.

As Major Jackson clambered onto the back seat of the open jeep beside Colonel Straight, he whispered into the colonel's ear. "I think we found our pilot, and she will make one hell of a traveling companion, if you know what I mean, sir."

"Major, I was going to pick her anyhow, but I was worried about how you would react to a female pilot. If you have other things in mind, I wish you luck, Major. Let's get her taken care of now." Turning to the driver and changing his volume and tone, the colonel bellowed at the driver. "Get this jeep to the hospital, Corporal."

The wind changed direction, and the acrid black smoke from the aviation fuel, the burning grass, and the smell of hot metal drifted across the jeep as the corporal made a sharp turn that almost threw Trudy out of the jeep, since her hands were starting to sting too much to hold on. The smoke stung Trudy's eyes and burned her nostrils. As the jeep moved out of the cloud of smoke, the clean, fresh air felt rejuvenating. In less than two minutes, they were at the aid station, and Trudy was rushed into the base hospital. An overzealous medic rushed to Trudy's side as she flopped down onto a stretcher. "Are you in pain, ma'am?" the medic inquired.

"My hands and knees hurt, but it's not serious."

Not waiting for more information, the medic anxiously injected Trudy with morphine from his side bag. Trudy felt warm and then went to sleep.

Trudy woke up a few hours later in a hospital gown with her hands and knees bandaged. Her good friend Shirley was sitting beside the bed.

"Hey, Trudy, how are yah feelin'?"

"That was some deep sleep; what time is it anyhow?"

"It's almost dinnertime. They said that you could leave after you woke up if you feel up to it."

Trudy moved her arms and legs and checked out the mobility of her hands and knees where they were bandaged.

"I'm fine. Did you drive all the way out here from Palm Springs?"

"No, I got a lift on a cargo flight. Carly and Toni were both flying today. When Carly told me what happened, I jumped on the next flight back to Mines Field. I saw what was left of that airplane of yours, and honey, you are so lucky that you didn't get burns. They said it was a total loss before they could get the fire out."

"I knew that I had to get out fast, which is why I ended up hands and knees on the pavement. I almost did a face-plant, too. That would have been less than deluxe."

"I'll tell the nurses you're up and getting ready to go while you get dressed. If you feel like it, we can pick up some burgers on the way back to your place so that you won't need to cook."

"Thanks, Shirley. I'll be ready in a couple of minutes."

Trudy got up, stretched, and started getting dressed. There was no way that she was spending the night in any hospital. Memories of her sister's long losing battle with breast cancer came back whenever she visited any hospital. As she finished getting dressed and looked in the mirror, Trudy realized that she had holes in the bloodstained fabric on her knees. The white bandages underneath showed through the tattered fabric, making them even more noticeable.

"Well, that's gonna look nice if we stop for burgers," Trudy said, pointing at her knees, as Shirley knocked and came back into the room.

"Do you want me to go get you some other clothes?"

"No, screw it. I just survived a plane crash, and I haven't eaten since breakfast, so people can stare all they want. Let's get out of here and get some food. My treat, Shirley."

"You know that you don't have to do that. OK, let's go. How about that diner just around the corner from your place?"

"You know that cook behind the counter is going to hit on you, so don't get mad, OK?"

"Get mad? Why do you think I suggested it? That surfer boy is really kinda cute."

"OK, we are off," Trudy said as she led the way out of the hospital.

"At least we get to have a little bit of fun tonight. I won't be able to stay around for the inevitable celebration, since I just got to check out on a new plane," Shirley said proudly.

"Oh, you are kidding? So they did let you fly that new A-26 Invader that you have been drooling over?"

"I'm flying one cross country, the day after tomorrow as pilot in command," Shirley said with the first big smile that Trudy had seen on her all afternoon.

"Shirley, that is wonderful. You just made my day!" Trudy said with sincere appreciation for her friend's new achievement.

CHAPTER 2
Malibu, California,
08 2145 January 1944

Trudy struggled with her matte red-lipstick tube, with her hands bandaged and fingers stiff. The pain in her palms from the missing skin was especially noticeable as she tried to put her fingers together and hold on to objects. Doorknobs were the worst.

"Just how long are you gonna be?" A western Pennsylvania accent erupted from the other side of the bathroom door.

"Oh, come on in. I'm just having a hell of a time trying to get my hands working so that I don't look like a clown tonight."

Toni Mazaro opened the bathroom door. "You're gonna look just fine. We've got a lot to celebrate tonight, and all the girls want to see you. That was some sweet landing, and everyone wants to know what happened and how you made it back because tomorrow that might just be us."

"Toni, I get it, but I'm still trying to figure out some of this myself. Everyone is acting like I'm some kind of hero for surviving, but what if something I did caused us to lose a plane?"

"They'll get to the bottom of it. The same thing that happened to you happened to Marty, and he didn't make it. You know how by the book he was, and he had more than twice the hours you got in Mustangs."

"I know, but they need to figure this out. I spent four hours yesterday getting debriefed on a fifteen-minute flight. We went over everything over and over and over again. As we went through this, the only thing that has changed is the fuel. I think it's that new fuel mixture they are using."

"Honey, me and the girls were talkin' last night, and we think it's the fuel, too. Rachel thinks some Jap saboteurs put something in the fuel," said Carly as she crowded into the bathroom doorway, accustomed to the stiff competition for bathroom time with her roommates.

"Rachel always blames the Japs since her brother got burned at Pearl Harbor. How could the Japs have done this? They are all in internment camps. More likely some second-generation German," Trudy said introspectively.

Carly burst into the bathroom past Toni, brush in hand, tending to her shoulder-length red hair as she rushed to the sink and jockeyed into position in front of the mirror, checking for lipstick on her teeth. "More likely war profiteers, diluting the gas to fuel their own cars. You two are so naïve. Not everyone is willing to sacrifice like we do. There are some old boys back home who do everything they can to stay on the home front so they can fuck beautiful girls like us while our boyfriends are fighting the war. That's one reason I won't even dance with a man who hasn't been in combat or isn't home on leave."

Toni put her hand on her hips and looked ready to dress down Carly. She paused for a moment with a stern look on her face before speaking. "Carly, you are so full of shit. You know damn well that you can get any man who lays eyes on you. Enjoy the moment. If you don't want to commit to one man, that's fine by me, but don't you cast aspersions on the rest of us."

Trudy stepped forward between Carly and Toni. "You two just stop. Enough. Now get out of here for a minute; I need to pee."

Carly and Toni both burst into laughter and stepped out of the bathroom, with Carly closing the door behind her. Trudy listened to her roommates giggle as she finished getting ready and exited the tiny bathroom. "OK, girls, let's get this party started," Trudy yelled and headed toward the front door.

Trudy had called for a car, and a Checker cab was waiting out in front of their apartment. Barely more than ten minutes later, the three roommates were dropped off at the door of Jimmy's Oceanside Club, not far from Malibu Beach.

Carly led the way into the rustic seaside bar, and Trudy immediately noticed the table in the back with twelve fellow WASPs. The stunningly beautiful trio received several approving smiles as Carly picked a circuitous path through the crowded bar. Most of the girls were already working on their second or third round of zombies—a rum drink served by the pitcher at Jimmy's.

There was an open spot at the head of the table with an empty glass and a pitcher of zombies. Toni ushered Trudy around the rowdy crowd and poured Trudy a full glass before taking a seat halfway down the table and asking the waiter for a Martini.

Carly grabbed a chair from the next table and pulled it in between Rachel and Trudy. After pouring a zombie and chugging half of it down, Carly stood back up and held up her glass: "To girls who fly and girls who die. Glad you made it this time, Trudy."

Trudy responded, standing but struggling to hold on to her glass. "To fly girls," she toasted as she smiled at her friends crowded around the table. "Thank you."

As everyone at the table sat back down, Carly leaned over to get closer to Trudy's ear.

"Did you see those four pilots at the table on the other side of the bandstand?" Carly said in a hushed voice, just loud enough for Trudy to hear her over the moderately loud jazz that the live band was playing.

"How could I miss them?" Trudy replied, glancing toward their table but quickly turning back to Carly as she caught the eye of movie-star handsome Major Gus Damon.

"Who is that hunk sitting next to Gus? I have never seen him before."

"That's Major Jackson. I met him after the crash happened. He rode with Colonel Straight out to the crash site."

"He is even better looking than Gus," Carly remarked with an evil smile that contrasted her bright white teeth against her dark red lipstick and freckled face.

"I think you are wrong about that. I also think he noticed you staring at him. He just got up and is heading this way," Toni injected into the conversation.

The three pretended not to notice Major Jackson's approach and attended to their drinks until a confident voice boomed from behind them.

"That was some pretty fine flying on Sunday, Miss Andrich. This must be the celebration party."

Trudy turned to acknowledge Major Jackson and again caught Major Damon's eye, long enough for him to give her a quick wink and get up. Trudy focused on Major Jackson again.

"Yes, Major Jackson, this is a celebration of sorts. The ladies at the table with me are all pilots here in Southern California. Most of them fly out of Mines Field like I do."

"Please call me Rod," Major Jackson said as he quickly surveyed the many beautiful and very fit women gathered around the long table.

"Rod? Is that your call sign? You really need to tell us how you got that name," Toni said with a wicked laugh.

"Actually, it is short for Roderick, but it is also my call sign," Rod replied staring straight into Toni's brown eyes with his blue eyes, which were famous for their ability to charm.

"I'll bet there is another story, too," Carly interjected.

"I'm sure Rod is too much of a gentleman to provide details," Trudy said seriously without even a hint of a smile.

Rod looked like he was about to reply when a hand appeared on his shoulder, and Gus moved from behind him. Gus stood close to Trudy, ignoring Rod and everyone else at the table.

"Is this Canuck bothering you?" Gus gestured toward Rod, whose blond hair stood out even more when standing next to Gus with his jet-black hair and neatly trimmed black mustache.

"What's a Canadian doing in the US Army Air Corps?" Trudy asked skeptically.

"I'm as American as he is," Rod replied. "I think Gus is referring to my service in the Canadian army, before the United States entered the war and while he was still making movies."

Carly and Toni looked even more impressed by the tall, blond, and athletic-looking pilot standing in front of them. Trudy's skeptical gaze remained on Gus.

"He wasn't bothering us; in fact he was being a very patient gentleman, in spite of the teasing he was getting from some of the ladies here at the table," Trudy glanced toward Toni and Carly who were both smirking.

Rod used the short exchange to get back on track.

"Trudy, would you like to dance?" Rod said confidently as he held out his hand to help Trudy up from the table.

"That is very sweet of you, Major, but having lost most of the skin on my knees, I am afraid that that would be a painful undertaking. I'm sure that Carly won't mind filling in for me, though."

Rod looked disappointed for a split second. "I understand," he said as he turned to Carly and held out his hand.

Carly was on her feet in a split second and was smiling from ear to ear as the two stepped away toward the small dance floor.

"Gus, why don't you sit down and have a drink?" Toni said as she pointed at Carly's now vacant seat.

"I would be delighted to."

Gus was quickly seated with his chair turned slightly toward Trudy. He motioned for the waiter. "Another bourbon and branch."

Turning back toward Trudy, Gus stared straight into her sky-blue eyes looking past the golden blond hair that framed her face. "You really dodged the bullet. Rod was just telling us about that amazing dead-stick landing that you pulled off."

"I just followed the script," Trudy said with a smile, knowing that Gus had been a Hollywood actor before the war interrupted his career.

"I would ask you to join me at my table, but I don't want to break up the celebration," Gus said sincerely.

"This won't last long. I have a meeting with Colonel Straight in the morning.

"Are you free tomorrow night? Maybe we can head out to that restaurant next to the pier and catch a movie afterward? I'm not flying for the next three days."

"That sounds great. You can pick me up at seven," Trudy replied.

"OK then. It's a date," Gus smiled.

"So what is all this about Major Jackson and the Canadian Army? Is that true?" Toni changed the subject.

Gus glanced back and forth between Trudy and Toni. "In fact it is true. Rod enlisted in the Canadian Army when he got frustrated at America's reluctance to join the war in Europe, before Pearl Harbor. He has English ancestry and thought that it was his duty to help out."

"So how did he end up in the Army Air Corps?" Trudy asked with a puzzled look.

"Rod ended up in the The Black Watch, Royal Highland Regiment of Canada, basically the Canadian Commandos. And if you remember Dieppe, it was a slaughter. Of the 556 men in his regiment, 200 were killed, and 264 were captured. Rod survived by jumping off a sea wall. Badly wounded he carried one of his buddies off the beach, and they were the only two survivors in his squad. He got a Victoria Cross for that, and when he finished his enlistment, he went home to New York City, thinking that the war was over for him. Instead there was a draft notice waiting."

"They drafted him after all of that?" Toni said incredulously.

"They sure did, but he said that he had enough of fighting in the infantry, so he volunteered for the Air Corps."

Carly and Rod appeared from behind Gus, with Carly looking a bit put off that Gus was in her seat and she could not grab her zombie without reaching awkwardly over him. Gus immediately picked up on her discomfort and shot to his feet.

He reached out for Trudy's hand as soon as he was on his feet and gave her willingly provided hand a quick kiss. "I'll pick you up at seven," he said to Trudy. "Carly, Toni, ladies, have a wonderful evening. I am afraid that I have been charged with getting our Canadian guest back to his quarters at a reasonable hour so that he can meet with Colonel Straight in the morning."

"Ladies, it has been a pleasure. Trudy, I will see you in the morning in Colonel Straight's office at 0700?"

"Yes, I guess so," Trudy said with a confused look, not expecting Rod to be at her meeting with the colonel.

Rod and Gus headed toward the door.

"Damn, that Rod has a nice ass," Carly said with admiration as she watched them depart.

"Have just a little bit of dignity," Toni teased. You are embarrassing Trudy."

"I know that she wasn't looking at Rod's ass as they walked away, so I just needed to give her full situational awareness," Carly said as her evil smile returned.

"Girls, I need to turn in soon. Apparently I have a meeting with Colonel Straight and Rod in the morning. I wonder why he needs to hear me brief Colonel Straight on the crash."

"Who knows? Maybe he is one of those FBI guys out here to investigate saboteurs? There is something fishy about him. I only danced with him for a couple of songs. And his hands were all over me, and he never once looked me straight in the eye. I'm telling you both he may have a nice ass, but I don't trust him," Carly said with a stern look and a suddenly lecturing tone.

"OK, let's finish these drinks and get out of here," Trudy said as she emptied the pitcher of zombies into her glass.

CHAPTER 3

Mines Field HQ, United States, 09 0645 January, 1944

Trudy walked toward the base headquarters at Mines Field feeling a bit foggy. Maybe it was the zombies or the residual effects from the morphine after the crash, but Trudy knew that she was not at the top of her game. That thought quickly passed as she started to think about what she would wear to her date with Gus and as she continued to stroll toward the base headquarters. After arriving just five minutes before her 0700 appointment with Colonel Straight, she entered the colonel's reception area and approached the orderly—a skinny and bored-looking young sergeant.

"Good morning, Sergeant, Trudy Andrich here to see Colonel Straight," Trudy said in a very formal tone.

"Take a seat. I'll let the colonel know that you're here," he said dismissively as he picked up the phone. "Sir, Miss Andrich is here to see you."

Before Trudy could sit down, Colonel Straight came out of his office. "Trudy, thank you so much for coming. How are you feeling? I mean from the crash, not the celebration I hear that they threw for you," Colonel Straight said, seeming slightly embarrassed.

"I'm fine, sir, from both ordeals," Trudy replied as she followed the colonel back into his office, noticing Major Jackson sitting very formally off to the side of Colonel Straight's desk.

"Trudy, I must admit that I was not completely honest with you when I asked you to attend this meeting. We will not be going over that superb flying performance you put on, but it certainly made it easier for some other reasons that I will soon provide."

Major Jackson spoke up for the first time.

"Trudy, before we can proceed, I must ask you to read and sign this secrecy agreement. Anything that we discuss here this morning can never be revealed to anyone not involved with Project Stinger." Major Jackson handed Trudy a clipboard with a secrecy agreement, which Trudy quickly read over and signed while Colonel Straight and Major Jackson quietly waited. She handed the clipboard back to Major Jackson. Major Jackson looked at the signature, added a date, and nodded to the colonel.

"Trudy, I have selected you for something very important, and, in fact, I believe you are the only pilot we have who is capable of succeeding. If you agree to take part in Project Stinger, your life will never be the same. If you decide you are not willing or able to participate, you will walk out that door and continue to be my best test and ferry pilot, and we will never discuss this meeting again. Are you willing to listen to Major Jackson's proposal?"

Trudy felt butterflies in her stomach. Maybe this was finally her chance to get into the war, she thought.

"Yes, sir, please tell me how I can help."

"Major Jackson, please proceed," Colonel Straight directed.

Rod stood up and walked over to the projector screen on the wall at the back of the colonel's office. He smoothly reached down and gave a quick tuck on the handle and let the screen retract into its spring-loaded roller, revealing a map of Europe.

"Trudy, we have built a special version of the P-51D here at the North American plant that will allow me to fly from England to Lithuania and rescue a scientist who must not fall into Russian hands or complete his research for the Germans. To carry out this mission, we have reduced the number of machine guns from six to two and increased the internal fuel capacity. Those guns each weigh just over sixty pounds, and the ammo load that we will save is another six hundred fifty pounds. Those changes alone will allow us to carry an extra thousand pounds of aviation gas, remembering that it weighs about six pounds per gallon. We have also removed some of the radio gear, shifted the fuselage tank, and added a second seat behind the pilot. There are two of these aircraft in the hangar at the end of the runway. One is a backup. I will be flying one of these planes from Duxford, England, seemingly participating in an escort mission for a B-17 bombing mission over Berlin. The difference is that instead of returning to Duxford with the rest of the escorts, I will be heading on to Kaunas, Lithuania, to meet up with the Lithuanian underground and fly our scientist back to Allied-controlled territory."

"So why do you need me?" Trudy asked skeptically.

"Well, it's pretty obvious how short we are on Army Air Corps fighter pilots, or as a woman you wouldn't be flying in the first place. You do seem like a competent pilot, for a woman. The modifications that we made to the Mustangs to allow them to fly all the way to Lithuania and back have made them handle a little bit differently. For an experienced male pilot, I don't think it would even be worth discussing, since they could figure it out," Major Jackson explained in a matter-of-fact tone.

"Moving fuel farther back into the fuselage has changed the balance of the aircraft. There have been some minor changes to the wings, too. It has made these planes unstable at low speed, Trudy, and if you fly them fast enough to handle like the planes that you normally fly, you will overheat the engine and probably run out of fuel a lot sooner," Colonel Straight interjected. "That's why we need you. Major Jackson has already flown these birds and has gotten used to the quirky way they can be handled. We need you to fly the backup plane with Major Jackson to Duxford, and since we don't want enemy eyes on these planes, we have a very unusual route planned."

"I'm in. If he can fly these planes, I can, too," Trudy said confidently. "I can fly it all the way to Lithuania, too, if you let me."

"I expected you to say that. Major Jackson will brief you on the detailed flight characteristics of the hybrids while I head over to check out the mess hall. Won't you Major Jackson? Trudy, your bags have already been packed for you, and your crew chief has loaded them on board your plane. I knew that you wouldn't turn this down," Colonel Straight said as he excused himself and started to leave Major Jackson and Trudy in his office.

"Sir, I need to make a few calls. I had plans tonight," Trudy said as she stood up.

"Trudy, I am afraid that you will not be making any calls. Remember I said that this mission would change your life. When you take off this afternoon, we will have you routed out over the ocean just before dusk.

You will call an in-flight emergency, and your Mayday call will lead everyone to believe that the fuel problem we have been having has gotten the better of you. When your mission is complete, we will have you return via Mexico, picked up by some Mexican fishermen at sea."

"And if something really happens?" Trudy said with a creased brow.

"Then you died at sea off the coast of California due to a fuel problem. Your aircraft and your remains will, of course, never be recovered," Major Jackson interrupted.

"I understand. Let's get started, Major Jackson."

"Please call me Rod."

CHAPTER 4
Mines Field, United States, 09 1700 January 1944

"**M**ustang flight, you are cleared for rolling and simultaneous take-off. Make right traffic, and maintain contact with Mines Field tower until feet wet. Contact Palm Springs tower when in sight. Also be advised that our radar has been out due to maintenance all after-noon," Lieutenant Busher said over the Mines Tower radio frequency.

"Mines Tower, this is Mustang flight leader. Cleared for rolling and simultaneous takeoff. Will make right traffic and contact Palm Springs when in sight," Major Jackson repeated back to the tower.

The two Mustangs thundered along the taxiway and onto the runway, and instead of stopping and running up the engine to max throttle, they continued their roll. And while maintaining barely minimum separation, they added power and were both in the air less than halfway down the runway. As they crossed the end of the runway, both aircraft turned and flew parallel to the runway until they crossed the beach and were flying above the Pacific Ocean.

"Mines Tower, this is Mustang flight; we are feet wet and switching to internal frequency."

With that call, Rod and Trudy switched their radio to their internal channel.

"OK, Trudy, remember to do exactly what I do, and maybe you won't need to return to the field with engine failure this time. You need to stay on me until we are out of sight of land, and then we can make our turn north instead of the turn south on the flight plan. Palm Springs will be calling us in as overdue about the same time we will be landing at Victorville Field."

"Roger, flight leader, I'll give you a five-minute head start as we planned so someone in Santa Clarita doesn't call in that they spotted two Mustangs flying together toward Palmdale when the news reports come out that we are overdue."

"I wonder how long they will search for us," Rod joked.

"That's gonna cost them some bucks," Trudy said with a forced laugh, since she was still angry from Rod's comments about returning to the field with engine failure. *What an asshole*, Trudy thought as she executed a flight maneuver.

"Don't worry, it comes out of the Coast Guard's budget instead of ours. We have another aircraft that is going to dump aviation gas out in the search area to form a slick. That will make it look like we had a midair collision, and they can call off the search faster. OK, Trudy, making my right turn now. I'll see you on the ground at Victorville."

"Roger, flight leader. I hear that Victorville is a real garden spot," Trudy quipped.

"Maybe if you like cactus and sidewinders. Mustang flight leader changing call sign to tail number now and switching to Victorville Tower frequency. They'll have the lights on for us."

CHAPTER 5
Malibu, California, 09 1900 January 1944

Major Gus Damon pulled up to the curb in front of Trudy's apartment in his dark-blue 1944 Packard sedan. In his excitement, he almost forgot to shut off the engine before he opened the door. He did not, however, forget the bouquet of flowers that he had picked up just around the corner and held it behind his back as he knocked on the door exactly at 7:00 p.m.

Toni answered the door expecting a man in uniform with bad news after noticing the sedan out front as she came to the door.

"Good evening, Toni, I think?"

Toni nodded but maintained a solemn expression.

"I'm here to see Trudy," Gus announced, still holding the flowers behind his back with his left hand.

"You'd better come in. Trudy is overdue," Toni exclaimed, holding back tears.

"From work, or...," Gus said incredulously as he lowered the bouquet and held it against his side.

"She was due at Palm Springs before six. She wasn't even supposed to be flying today, but she had a last-minute ferry run to Palm Springs in a two ship with Major Jackson."

"I knew he was leaving today. What do they think happened?"

"Lieutenant Busher called asking if we had heard from her. He said that they were last seen flying due west over the ocean and that they never contacted Palm Springs Tower. The radar was out for maintenance, so no one is sure, but they suspect a midair collision and will start looking for life rafts as soon as it is light."

"Wow, when it rains, it pours. I wonder if it was the fuel problem again. Maybe they had to ditch. No big surf today, so they might be OK."

"Can I get you a drink?" Carly said as she entered the room. She had one in hand for herself already, and her mascara revealed her recent tears.

"No, thanks, just put these in water," Gus said as he handed Carly the bouquet. "I'm heading out to the base. They can probably use an extra pilot for the search."

Gus rushed out the door and jumped into his car. He squealed the tires of his powerful car as he pulled away from the curb and headed toward the base.

CHAPTER 6
Victorville Field, United States, 10 0600 January 1944

"It's a cold morning. I'm glad that they kept our planes inside the hangar last night," Trudy said with her breath steaming as she spoke. She crossed her arms as she walked beside Rod toward the hangar.

"Just like a woman to complain about the cold. We're lucky it's cold; that keeps the rattlesnakes in the ground. On hot days, they hide in the shade under the airplanes, and when it's warm at night, they sometimes crawl up the landing gear into the wheel wells. If you ask me, the only time it's fit to be out here is when it is cold."

Trudy chose to ignore Rod's insult. The hangar doors were already open, and Trudy noticed that their two Mustangs were the only planes inside. A P-40 Warhawk and some C-47 Skytrains were parked outside the hangar, wheels chocked. The thick frost on their wings indicated that they had been there all night. As Trudy started the preflight check on her plane, she immediately noticed that the plane had been worked on while they slept.

"They installed our guns last night," Trudy yelled out to Rod, who was already inspecting his plane.

"They sure did, and they have the ammo loaded, too. Don't shoot me down, OK?" Rod said only half joking.

"Don't worry; I have flown these birds with all six Brownings installed, and I'm not a bad shot either."

"Why did they let a female ferry pilot do gunnery? That seems like a waste of ammo to me," Rod said with a slightly disgusted look.

"I am also a test pilot, and guns are one of the things I test. You don't want some green fly-boy to find out in the middle of a dogfight that his guns are installed wrong, do you?"

"I guess that makes sense. Sorry," Rod replied and went back to his preflight checklist.

Soon checks were complete, and Trudy joined Rod next to his plane. Rod handed her a small notebook.

"Trudy, we have flight plans in place now for the rest of our trip. Today we are headed to Colorado Springs, Colorado. We'll call that Day 1. On Day 2 we fly from Colorado Springs to Saint Louis, Missouri. On Day 3 we fly from Saint Louis to Franklin, Pennsylvania."

"Where the hell is Franklin?"

"It is just about a hundred miles north of Pittsburg. It's in the middle of nowhere, which is why we chose it." Rod paused and looked up at Trudy suddenly noticing her wrapping her long blond hair into a bun. "Are you even listening to me?" Rod exclaimed, partly to hide his reason for staring.

"Yes, I'm listening. Trust me; I do this at least once a day, and it doesn't require much thought. So, from Franklin where do we go?"

"Day 4 is a rest day, and while we enjoy the solitude of Franklin, they'll give the planes a good going over. On Day 5, we head to Halifax, Nova Scotia, which will be one of our first long-range flights. That will be a tough day for us and the planes, but it is better to find out if we have a problem now instead of over the Atlantic. On Day 6, we will head to Nuuck, Greenland, which will be a relatively short flight, but we will need to rest up and top off our fuel tanks before we head from Greenland to Duxford, England, on Day 7. Any questions?"

"I thought that Greenland belonged to Denmark? Aren't they helping the Germans?" Trudy asked.

"Denmark does own Greenland, but we have a small contingent of US troops there now to occupy parts of it. The Germans tried a couple of times to establish outposts there. Most of them surrendered without a fight when we arrived and cut off their supplies. There are probably spies there, too, but we won't leave the base. Trust me, you will not want to."

"How does the weather look?" Trudy said with a worried expression. "I hear that they get a lot of snow in northwestern Pennsylvania this time of year."

"Just wait until you see Greenland this time of year. We could literally be stuck there for weeks if the weather turns bad. Ah, that reminds me, have you ever landed in the snow?"

Trudy hesitated a moment before she answered: "Not yet, and hopefully I never will."

"Oh, you will, if not in Nova Scotia, you will in Greenland."

Determined to make the rest of the long trip to Duxford more cordial, Trudy changed the subject.

"I always wondered why they called it that. I have heard a number of explanations," Trudy said introspectively.

"Well, maybe you can ask someone when you get there. Speaking of getting there, let's get going. We have a long flight today. On the plus side, we get a great view of the Rocky Mountains. They are expecting mountain snow tonight, but today we have clear skies, and Colorado Springs barely ever gets much snow. When it does snow there, it melts away fast."

"I'm looking forward to seeing Pikes Peak. My dad always told me stories about racing up Pikes Peak when he was a young man. He said that they didn't win, but it was one of the most memorable days of his life."

"I guess that I am not surprised that the father of a woman pilot would be a race-car driver. Did he do that professionally while you were growing up?"

"No, he was an investment banker, and I didn't see much of him for weeks at a time as he traveled around the world. When he was home, there was no better father."

"I'll bet he is proud of you now," Rod said with a smile.

"He passed away while I was in WASP training in Texas. My mom died the year before, and it broke his heart. They had been together since college. What about your family?"

"My father was a raging alcoholic who ran off with a new woman every month. My mother tolerated it because of the benefits of having a rich husband, and she wanted the best for me. When I went away, she killed herself, and my father married my widowed aunt who I never got along with."

"I'm sorry."

"Don't be. I had a very privileged upbringing. In high school my parents sent me to the New York Military Academy; after that I attended Harvard."

This probably explains why he acts like such a jerk, Trudy thought.

"You had to be bright to get into Harvard," Trudy said to try to compliment Rod.

"Actually, my grades at the military academy were atrocious. I got in because of a large donation my father had made the year that I applied for admission. He thought that I didn't know about that. The wind is picking up; we need to get going. I do think you will like where we are staying tonight. It's a hotel called the Broadmoor, not far from the airfield."

"That sounds better than a barracks. Let's go," Trudy said as she jogged off toward her airplane to warm up.

CHAPTER 7

Franklin, Pennsylvania, 15 0800 January 1944

"So, any sign of the weather clearing?" Trudy asked with an air of resignation as she entered the pilots' lounge at base operations. "Maybe by late tonight. We have a chance of getting out of here in the morning before another lake effect front comes through early afternoon with more snow," Rod answered quickly, interrupted by Trudy as he took the first sips of his first black coffee of the morning.

"Well, that's just jim-dandy, isn't it? So we get to spend another day in this winter wonderland," Trudy said with an air of disgust.

"Well, that was the bad news. The good news is that I got us a ride into Franklin for lunch. In about an hour, they are sending a deuce-and-a-half six-by-six with chains on into town for supplies, and you and I are on the manifest."

"How did you work that out?" Trudy said in a very surprised tone.

"I think the base-ops guys are sick of you bitching about the weather all day," Rod said as he held back a chuckle.

"Oh, and I suppose that they enjoy your singing so much that you had to bribe them to allow you to leave," Trudy said very sarcastically.

"Hmm. That would mean that you owe me a drink, maybe two, when we get into town."

"If you get me out of here today, I will gladly buy as many drinks as it takes to get you drunk, but remember, we are flying out of here tomorrow. Right?"

"I already arranged for portable space heaters to get the hangar above freezing and every gallon of ethylene glycol in Venango County for getting us deiced after run-up. I am not particularly fond of this place, either. But one last thing. We will be riding in the back of the deuce-and-a-half, so you better go back to your room and get your flight gear on, and don't forget your long johns."

"That still works for me. I'll meet you back here in an hour."

Trudy and Rod both hurried back to their rooms, and after struggling with extra pairs of socks and other minor clothing issues, they were ready for, at the very least, a minor adventure, and just possibly a good meal and a few beers.

An hour later, Trudy and Rod met back at base operations, where a couple of young enlisted GIs were greedily gulping down the free coffee in the pilots' lounge.

"So, are you the two Eskimos who want to ride in the back of our truck all the way into town?" the twenty-five-year-old corporal, who seemed to be in charge, asked as he slurped his full mug of coffee without getting up.

"Major Jackson and I are the two Eskimos you are looking for," Trudy said shrewdly.

The corporal jumped to his feet, spilling his coffee. He quickly turned to the private lounging next to him with a canteen cup full of coffee. "Get up, you moron; don't you know how to behave when an officer enters the room?" The corporal quickly turned back to the major and saluted. "Sir, I apologize for my driver's behavior. Would the lady like to sit up front with us? It will be a bit warmer…"

"Corporal, I think that unless the front seat fits four, this pilot and I will be sitting in the front seat, and you will be sitting in the back."

The corporal dropped his salute. "Sir, my driver is very new, and I can't let him drive you down Route 8 in the snow without supervision, so he will sit in back, and I will drive us to Franklin."

"And back here before dark?" Trudy interjected.

"Yes, ma'am, we'll get back here around three before it ices up too bad. The way back is all uphill."

"So, if you are driving, why does the private even need to come?" Rod asked.

"Well, sir, to help load the truck," the corporal said sheepishly.

"I'll tell you what, when we get downtown, I'll make sure the crew at the warehouse will load the truck for you and then you drop us off where we can get some lunch and a few beers. Private, you stay here until I get back under my orders, and don't let any of that coffee go to waste, OK?"

The private broke into a big smile before saluting smartly. "Yes, sir. Thank you, sir."

"Corporal, let's be on our way," Rod said as he led the way to the door. The sidewalk in front of the small fixed-base operations office had been shoveled, but snow had been compressed into ice wherever there was a footprint. All three seemed to be performing an awkward dance as they gingerly stepped between the icy footprints to tread on the half inch of new snow for better traction. It was well below zero, and the snow squeaked beneath their feet. The corporal led the way to the big olive-drab deuce-and-a-half, parked across the parking lot, which had been recently plowed and peppered with cinders to provide traction.

All three travelers climbed into the front cab, and the corporal cranked the motor, which made a sickening groan but did not start. On the second attempt, the big motor came to life, and the truck shuddered like a bear waking up from a winter slumber.

The chains attached to the double set of dual wheels in the back of the truck provided more than adequate traction, and the truck felt more like a barge as it plowed forward through almost half a foot of new snow blanketing Route 8. They made slow but steady progress as they descended on the serpentine two-lane road into town.

"So, where are you from, ma'am?" the corporal asked as he avoided a snow plow that was headed up the hill.

"Southport, Connecticut," Trudy replied.

"I have to say, ma'am, that I am surprised. I had you pegged for be'n a Southern girl. Since you are a pilot and such. The corporal looked puzzled.

"I'm a little bit insulted that you think us New England girls could or wouldn't want to fly a plane. Truth is, though, I used to spend summers on my uncle's farm in Tidewater, Virginia, so maybe you picked up on the slight accent that I picked up down there. So, where are you from, Corporal?" Trudy replied.

"West by God Virginia, ma'am, which is why driving through all this snow here in Pennsylvania is just a walk in the woods."

"So, where did you learn how to fly, if you don't mind my asking, Connecticut or Virginia?" Rod asked.

"Actually several places. I learned to fly the army way in Sweetwater, Texas. I spent most of my free time sailing while I was in Connecticut. But one day down in Virginia, I was watching a crop duster fly back and forth over my uncle's tobacco fields, and my uncle told me that the wings on an airplane worked just like a sail. And the light bulb came on, and I knew that someday I needed to sail across the sky like I did across the water."

"Wings work like a sail?" The corporal looked perplexed.

"Most people think that wind fills a sail and pushes a boat."

"Ain't that how it works?" the corporal interrupted.

"If that was true, a sailboat could never go faster than the speed of the wind. Instead, the wind fills the sail and gives it a curved shape like a wing. The wind moving across the curved side of the sail creates lower pressure on that side of the sail and pulls the boat forward," Trudy explained.

"Well, I'll be damned. Makes perfect sense when you explain it that way. So that's how wings lift airplanes. I always thought it was wind reflecting off the bottom of the wing. I'll be damned." The corporal smiled and nodded, proud of his newfound insight.

"So, to answer your question, I learned to fly crop dusters in Virginia and got my pilot's license. The WASPs only accepted women who already had a license, but then they taught us how to fly military airplanes in Texas."

"I'll bet we sailed some of the same waters in Connecticut, Trudy. I learned to sail at a day camp on Long Island. On a breezy summer day, there must have been a hundred sailboats on Long Island Sound," Rod commented.

The conversation was interrupted as the corporal downshifted and slid the truck around a sharp right-hand turn. The street ahead was lined with shops and looked typical of any small town in America. The sidewalks were all swept clean of snow, and people went about their business seemingly oblivious to the cold and snow.

The corporal continued through town. Avoiding parked cars along the curb, he pointed out a couple of places to eat on the right-hand side of the street. Passing the courthouse and a few blocks later several large churches, the buildings changed to a more industrial look, and just before a bridge, there was a warehouse with an American flag flying out front. The corporal pulled the truck into the parking lot and backed up to the loading dock. The three made ungraceful exits from the cab onto the pavement.

"OK, we're here," the corporal announced.

A bored-looking young second lieutenant peered through the window of the door next to the loading dock and reluctantly stepped outside.

"Are you here for the airport pickup?" the lieutenant said as he glanced over a clipboard.

"Yes, sir. I hear that Betty Grable needs a ride to the airport," the corporal goaded the lieutenant.

"That's enough of that, Private," the lieutenant barked back, not ready to put up with any hint of insubordination.

"Them's corporal stripes, sir," the corporal said, pointing to his shoulder.

"Those might not be there by the time you leave here if you don't explain what a dame is doing in your truck," the lieutenant said as he pointed at Trudy. "I don't think she is Betty Grable, either," he added.

"Lieutenant, I'm Major Jackson, and this pilot is Miss Andrich. She is a WASP pilot ferrying a military aircraft. We've been weathered in at the airport, and the corporal gave us a ride into town for some lunch. You are welcome to join us after you have your men load up this truck," Rod added slyly.

"Sir, I didn't expect an officer." The lieutenant smartly saluted, and Rod returned his salute. "I can't leave here until all the delivery drivers finish up today, but there is a good place called Franky's just about two blocks away on your left heading back into town. You can easily walk there, and the corporal can pick you up after we load him up and inventory the load. A lot of the guys here go there after work, so the path is pretty clear the whole way there."

"That's a great idea, Lieutenant. If you change your mind, you are still welcome to join us."

The lieutenant saluted again. "Thank you, sir. I'll have the corporal pick you up at Franky's in a little over an hour. Enjoy your lunch, sir and ma'am.

Trudy allowed Rod to lead the way since the path was cleared only one snow shovel wide. After a ten-minute walk, they crossed the street, and Rod held open the door of Franky's, a small bar with the feel of an old English pub.

"Sit anywhere you want," a booming voice said from behind the bar.

Trudy led the way to the bar and popped up onto one of the bar stools. Rod adjusted his stool, tilting it a little bit toward Trudy, and then sat down beside her.

"The menu is on the chalkboard behind me. The soup of the day is vegetable we made with our own canned tomatoes," the tall, muscular, gray-haired, and balding bartender announced.

"I'll have the soup with a grilled cheese sandwich," Trudy said. "Oh, and what do you have on tap?"

"We got Schlitz, Miller, Yuengling, and Rolling Rock. We're all out of Budweiser until the end of the week."

"I'll have a Miller."

"Miller, grilled cheese, and vegetable soup for the lady. What can I get you, Major?"

"Schlitz and a burger along with that soup."

"Schlitz and burger with another soup," the bartender yelled toward the kitchen as he turned around to grab a couple of glasses and work the taps.

"So, talk is all over town that a woman flew a Mustang pursuit plane into the airport a few days ago. That wouldn't be you, would it?" the bartender said as he pointed at Trudy's flight jacket.

"Yes, I guess that's me, unless there are more Mustangs at Franklin Airport that I don't know about," Trudy said with a big smile.

"We got a girl from the next town over, Oil City, who flies Mustangs out in California. Her old man was in the big war with me, so he talks about her all the time over at the Legion Hall. Toni's her name."

A horrified look came over Rod's face as he listened to the exchange.

"I don't think I know her," Trudy lied. "There are quite a few of us flying now, and we are spread all over the country."

"Yah, I suppose so. Well, if you ever run into her, you can say you were right across the river from her hometown. Her full name's Toni Mazaro. She's a good Italian girl: tall, slender, with big brown eyes just like her mom. That's what her old man always says. He misses her like the dickens."

Rod relaxed as Trudy maintained their thin cover story, at least for the time being. A tough-looking woman with a stained apron worn over a homemade checked dress emerged from the back with a plate in each hand.

"The major gets the burger," the bartender said, pointing.

"I know he gets the burger. I was only ten feet away when you bellowed their orders back to me. I was already workin' on them by the time you yelled," the woman said sarcastically.

"It's just a habit from when it gets busy and you can't hear over all the noise," the bartender said apologetically.

"It ain't been busy in here since the war started." The woman waved dismissively and headed back to the kitchen.

"She's right about that, I guess. Not like it used to be here. We got some skilled fellas over at the Joy plant making tank parts; some of us vets from the last war who are too old are here, too, along with the sick, lame, and lazy. The rest of the fellas are over in Europe unless they were German descent, and in that case, they sent those boys to the Pacific to fight the Japs."

"That's funny in a weird sort of way. On the West Coast, they are sending volunteers from the Japanese internment camps to fight the Germans," Trudy said.

"I heard about them internment camps. Don't seem right, but look how them Japs sneak attacked us. I guess Roosevelt knows best," the bartender said introspectively.

"Do you have a son over there?" Rod asked. "I noticed the blue star in the window."

"I sure do. My boy was in the 28th Infantry Division with most of the rest of the guys from around here, and then he got the wild idea that he needed to volunteer for the airborne. I guess he likes airplanes, too. He just don't get to fly 'em."

"Airborne. Wow, he must be one tough young man," Trudy said with admiration.

"He always was a good athlete, good with the grades, too. I think that's why they made him a sergeant so fast," the bartender said with a lot of pride. "He already done better than me. I stayed a private the whole time I was in."

"He's a good boy, too," the woman in the back yelled out from the kitchen.

"Look who's yelling now," the bartender said, shaking his head. You done with those plates? Ready for another beer?"

Trudy and Rod both nodded with their mouths full.

"Sure. We'll have another round. Our ride won't be here for another twenty minutes," Rod said, looking at the Breitling watch on his wrist as he pulled up the sleeve of his flight jacket, which normally covered the watch.

Trudy glanced at his watch, understanding how expensive it was. She was surprised that Rod was wearing it, but she decided not to comment and took another sip of beer instead.

Before they could finish their second round, the corporal arrived to take them back up the hill to the airport.

"The truck is all warmed up for you two, sir," the corporal said, awkwardly adding the word *sir* almost as an afterthought.

Rod took care of the check. After shaking hands with the bartender and a couple of farewell shouts back to the kitchen, the three were on their way.

"Looks like it's finally clearing up," Trudy said, pointing at the first piece of blue sky she had seen in days.

"That it is. We'll get out of here tomorrow, just like the weather service predicted," Rod said, looking approvingly skyward.

Trudy glanced over at Rod for a moment. *Maybe this guy is not so bad when you get to know him*, Trudy thought.

CHAPTER 8
Halifax, Nova Scotia,
16 0800 January 1944

It had been a tough flight to Halifax. Icing conditions and turbulence had worn out Trudy both mentally and physically. Her Mustang was safely parked inside a hangar, and now Trudy trudged along the snow-covered path to the Quonset hut where she would spend the night. The snow reflected the moonlight, which provided just enough light to make out the pathway. There was more than six feet of snow piled on either side. *At least the snow is deep enough to block the wind*, Trudy thought. The landing had been difficult in a twenty-mile-per-hour cross-wind, gusting at times to almost twice that. The icy wind on the fully exposed ramp had been biting, seeming to cut right through her flight suit. She wished that she could have taxied straight into the hangar, but ground crews and tugs were waiting on the ramp. The ground crew also provided heavy winter parkas to both pilots almost as soon as their feet hit the ground.

Trudy and Rod were quickly herded into canvas-covered jeeps. Trudy noticed that a Canadian officer was riding with Rod and that they headed off in the opposite direction from the row of Quonset huts used to house visiting flight crews. Maybe they were headed off to check on the weather? Trudy thought it was strange that they headed off without saying a word. Something just didn't feel right.

Once inside her quarters, Trudy was surprised to find a stack of magazines and pulp-fiction novels filling a small bookcase next to a narrow wooden desk. Trudy chuckled as she uncovered a copy of *Life* magazine from July 1943, with WASP pilot Shirley Slade on the cover. After spending a few minutes going through the unexpected treasures, Trudy settled on a mystery novel that seemed to still have all the pages: *Murder on the Orient Express* by Agatha Christie.

"That sounds interesting," Trudy said out loud.

She kept her jacket on. The steam heat was on, but the galvanized steel arching over her to form the hut was uninsulated except for the snow that covered it.

As Trudy settled in for the night with her book, the phone rang. Trudy threw off the blanket and grabbed for the phone.

"Hello," she said with surprise in her voice, not having noticed the phone as she settled in.

"Takeoff time is 1000. The weather looks good. I'll call and wake you up around 0800 so that we can catch breakfast," Rod instructed.

"OK, that sounds fine. So breakfast at 0830?"

"If you can get ready that fast," Rod said skeptically.

"I don't think I need to spend very much time with my makeup, unless breakfast is a formal affair. I'll be ready," Trudy fired back.

"OK, mess hall at 0830. Good night."

The next morning, when the wake-up call came at 0800, Trudy was already almost fully dressed. The hut was cold enough that Trudy could see her breath. *It must be a hundred below outside,* she thought as she repacked her flight bag. By 0815, Trudy had her parka zipped up and was headed out the door toward the mess hall. She tried to ignore the cold since she knew that it would be even colder at twenty thousand feet. The gusts of wind refused to let her forget, though, and she shivered again. After a ten-minute walk, Trudy entered the relative warmth of the mess hall and hung her parka on the long coat rack near the door.

Cat calls rang out as Trudy entered the mess hall, which wasn't at all unusual. Trudy also recognized Rod's voice saying something about "getting into her pants" and looked in the direction of the conversation. She noticed that the Canadian officer she had seen with Rod the day before was sitting with Rod having a cup of coffee, so she walked over to their table before getting in line for food.

"Good morning, Trudy. Please let me introduce you to Squadron Leader Eric Rice," Rod said as he and Eric stood up to greet Trudy.

"I am charmed, madam; it's a great pleasure to meet such a fine pilot. Rod was just telling me how gifted you are with a stick and rudder pedals. Perhaps we can fly together someday."

"I think I might enjoy that, Squadron Leader Rice. What do you fly?"

"Please call me Eric. I fly Catalinas currently, supporting our U-Boat hunters escorting the North Sea convoys. Pretty boring stuff most of the time I'm afraid."

"Have you eaten yet?" Trudy said, changing the subject. "We, too, have a long boring flight today."

"We just had coffee. We were waiting for you to join us. Rod and I served in the Black Watch, Royal Highland Regiment, of Canada together. When he heard that I was flying, he thought it sounded like a pretty good idea, and he volunteered for flight school, too."

"You don't have a Canadian accent. Are you American, too?" Trudy asked as she tried to place the accent.

"I'm Canadian, but my father worked in Boston, and I went through grade school and high school there. I must admit I do love the Red Sox, too."

"Your Boston accent is subtle, but now that you mention it, I do recognize it coming through just a little bit."

"Oh, you should hear me when I'm drinking. I sound like I grew up next to Fenway."

"Oh, you mean like last night after you picked me up at the airfield? I don't understand how you got out of bed this morning," Rod exclaimed.

"You just reminded me that I really need to eat soon. Let's get some food," Eric said as he got up and led the way toward the chow line.

"So, tell me, Trudy, what are your plans after you get to England? Will you have a chance to stick around a bit? Now that we control the skies, there is just the occasional unexploded bomb to worry about."

"I think that I will need to head back as soon as possible. There are a lot of people who have no idea what happened to me," Trudy said in a very serious tone.

"Right, well there is that. It does seem like quite an opportunity if you just wanted to start over. I am sure that you could work something out if you decide you wanted to stay. I hear that they need women with your skills."

"Thank you, Eric. I'll keep that in mind, but there is a lot of work for me to do back home."

After filling their plates in the chow line, the three returned to the table, and Eric was questioned about conditions between Halifax and Greenland. On a cold morning like this, Trudy would normally have gulped down several cups of coffee in the course of an hour-long breakfast, but with a long flight ahead, she limited herself to two and noticed that Rod was doing the same.

The lengthy talk with Eric about the route also helped with some of the nagging nervousness Trudy was starting to have about such a long overwater flight in unusually harsh conditions. She knew that if they had to ditch, the cold water would paralyze them in seconds, and they would almost surely drown before they could climb into a life raft.

With breakfast finished, Trudy and Rod bid farewell to Eric and headed off to base operations, where they filed their flight plans and received a last-minute weather update from some recent flight reports. The preflight routine was fast, with Trudy and Rod setting the same pace and finishing at roughly the same time.

Within an hour they were airborne with the promised blue skies above. Those blue skies would not last long. This time of year there was less than five hours of daylight in Greenland, and it would be almost dark by the time they planned to arrive. They were expecting packed snow and ice on the runway. They both knew how challenging this would be for them and how tough it would be on the planes. If they blew a tire during landing, they might be there for weeks.

For safety, they planned to fly high above the water at twenty-five thousand feet. The extra altitude would give them time to react if something went wrong. As Trudy climbed through nineteen thousand feet on the way to her planned altitude, she felt the second stage of the Mustang's supercharger kick in, noticing a subtle surge in power. An amber indicator light lit up next to the word *high* beside the manual supercharger control. It was the Mustang's supercharger that allowed the plane to easily fly to thirty-five thousand feet, where comparable German airplanes without a supercharger would starve for oxygen in the thin, high-altitude atmosphere. At this altitude Trudy's oxygen mask was adjusted to fit tightly over her mouth and nose since her life now depended on the plane's onboard supply of compressed oxygen.

There was another reason to fly high; as Trudy looked south, a convoy of ships was heading due east, and Trudy watched with amazement as US Navy destroyers raced back and forth near a ship that was stopped and on fire. Above the destroyers at less than ten thousand feet above the water were two PBY Catalinas, like the one flown by Eric. Trudy had the urge to tune the radio and listen for his voice. The scene seemed surreal. Below, men might be drowning in the water, and a U-boat was lurking. At the speed that Rod and Trudy were traveling, the show did not last long, and in less than five minutes, the battle raged on behind them.

"It's a shame that we couldn't lend a hand." Rod's voice crackled over the radio.

"Let's maintain radio silence," Trudy said in a businesslike tone, suddenly realizing that weather was not the only threat to their safety.

After flying for another hour, Rod sighted land ahead, and their navigation had brought them close to their intended target in Greenland. Rod led Trudy on a slow descent that he calculated would allow them to make land if one of them had engine trouble. Twenty minutes later, the small American base established at the mouth of a fjord was revealed as they crossed over a mountain range at approximately fifteen thousand feet. Trudy stared at the scene below, seeing at least five airplanes including a B-17 that had been bulldozed off the end of the runway. Outside of the base, thousands of fuel barrels were scattered across the snow in random piles, abandoned there to rust. Inside the perimeter of the small base, there were fifteen or so small trucks that could have been delivered to the isolated fjord only by air. Two Quonset huts and what appeared to be four wooden-barracks buildings, with black smoke streaming out of one of the chimneys, were dangerously close to the runway.

"I don't see a tower to contact," Trudy questioned Rod.

"The tower is the corner office in the building closest to the runway. A real tower would get blown over in the persistent gales. This is a nice day, and look at that wind sock. I hope you are ready for a crosswind landing."

"Go ahead. Lead the way. You've been here before."

"Yah, I've been here, but I was a passenger. Please, be my guest. I'll circle and watch for polar bears on the runway."

"Oh, you are kidding, right?"

"I wish I was. They told me a story about how a polar bear attacked one of the P-51Bs right after landing to try and eat the pilot. The pilot ran across the ice emptying his pistol at the bear, which continued to tear apart the airplane to see if there was anything else in there to eat. That plane is still near the end of the runway, and you can see how effective polar-bear claws are on aircraft aluminum when you taxi past. Just don't slow down too much."

"Don't worry. I won't."

"OK, making right traffic at twelve hundred feet to check out the winds. You are right, it looks bad," Trudy said over the radio as she flew parallel to the runway. "Those are close to forty-knot gusts. You know we aren't supposed to land in these conditions."

"Now do you understand why there are all the junked planes at the end of the runway?"

"Yep, and I'm not gonna be one," Trudy said, and she circled once more and lined up for a long final approach.

Trudy kept her speed well above normal landing speed and still had the Mustang crabbing into the wind by almost forty-five degrees. She banked slightly to the right before contact, making sure that the upwind landing gear struck first. Trudy hit hard enough that without the blown snow over the metal corduroy landing strip she would probably have blown a tire. With both main gear on the ground Trudy stuck the tail to the ground with full back pressure on the stick as she applied the brakes hard. She felt the tires slide across the ice, and she slowed enough to turn around at the end of the runway. Trudy taxied back to midfield, not taking time to look at the damaged plane at the end of the runway for bear claw marks. At midfield Trudy pulled forward to a parking area near the building closest to the edge of the runway. As soon as the propeller stopped, three men in parkas ran out to the Mustang. Two of the men started tying down the airplane while the other man looked around cautiously.

Trudy climbed out of the Mustang and watched as Rod made a hard landing on the second bounce after flying the same pattern as Trudy.

"So, are the Germans that close?" Trudy yelled over the howling wind to the man with the shotgun.

"Germans? They are up on the northeast coast, hundreds of miles from here. This twelve-gauge is for polar bears. There ain't a lot for them to eat around here besides us."

Trudy immediately looked around for bears, and the man with the shotgun chuckled.

"Hey, that was a nice landing, but you better get inside before you freeze your ass off," the man with the shotgun said and pointed to the door. Trudy ran toward the door as the man who looked after her still waited on Rod to taxi up. "And freezing that ass off would be one hell of a waste," the man commented to himself as Trudy made it safely inside. There was a metal space heater inside with the chimney pipe glowing orange from overuse. And it was probably fifty degrees inside.

"It smells like aviation fuel in here," Trudy commented.

"You got that one right, miss," a heavy supply sergeant in his twenties replied. "They normally run those stoves on diesel. It's a lot safer, but diesel freezes into jelly here, so all they bring in is aviation gas by the drum. That's all we got for heat unless we start tearing these buildings apart and using them for heat. We already ripped up every other floorboard upstairs to board up the windows and keep the bears out. Watch out if they put you up there tonight; it's easy to fall through and break a leg."

The door opened, and a blast of cold air came in. Rod led the way followed by the two tie-down men, and the man with the shotgun came in last.

"Man, it is cold out there, and it's gonna get far worse before it gets better. Youze are lucky that you got in when you did," the man with the shotgun said as he pulled off his parka, revealing a silver first-lieutenant bar on his collar. He appeared to be in his late thirties.

"Who is in charge here, Lieutenant?" Rod said with a polite tone.

"Well, that would be me, Lieutenant Bridger. I am officially on orders as the base commander. I might be the lowest-ranking commander in the whole army," he said with a laugh.

"Yah, but you're the oldest," the supply sergeant yelled back and laughed.

"We wuz expecting you, sir. They told us to keep it a secret—like we had people to talk to. We get mail only once a month, when our supply planes come in. Half the time, like today, the radio don't even work 'cause of the northern lights, they tell me."

"So, how did you end up with this command? There has to be a story behind that," Rod asked.

"I know what you are thinking: an old lieutenant like me must have been busted down and sent here for really fucking up bad. That ain't the case, though. I actually volunteered to come here from Alaska. I was a corporal in the infantry back there. With a last name like Bridger, I had something to live up to. You heard of Jim Bridger, ain't you?"

"Yes, I have a book about him, an amazing fellow that also had a few run-ins with bears as he explored the West."

"All right, you do know," the lieutenant said with a smile.

"But you said that you were a corporal?" Rod continued.

"Yes, and after I got here, I made sergeant. Our base commander was a captain, and he got appendicitis and died before they could get him out, so I was in charge. A few months later, some generals had to put down here due to the weather and got stuck here for almost three weeks. So, to make a long story short, after the three-star saw how I was takin' care of things, he asked me if I wanted a job working for him."

"Why didn't you do that?" Trudy said somewhat incredulously.

"I told him that these were better conditions than what I grew up in back in Alaska, and I preferred to stay. He told me that in that case, I was now the permanent base commander, but he didn't have the authority to make me a captain, so I had to settle for being a first lieutenant."

"So, how long have you been here?" Rod said somewhat in awe.

"Two years now, goin' on three."

"Good for you! It looks like you found your niche in life," Trudy commented appreciatively.

"This isn't a niche, miss. This is a fjord," the lieutenant said with a straight face.

Trudy was speechless for a moment, and the lieutenant enjoyed the joke.

"You are right. I did find my niche. I was just joking with you a little bit. Now, are you folks hungry? Officially, all we got are C rations, but we've been stocking up smoked fish and even some bear meat. That's probably why the bears are trying to get in here all the time."

"Smoked fish with C rations will be great," Rod replied.

"I'll try some of the bear. I have had black bear at a hunting camp in Maine with my father. I wasn't a big fan of it, but I wasn't this hungry, either," Trudy added.

"OK, then we will get you settled upstairs where it is probably twenty degrees warmer than it is down here. After that, we'll eat. I'm afraid that we may need to dig your planes out in the morning after the storm passes through tonight. As cold as it is, it will be powder, so don't worry about the weight on your airplanes. You already passed the toughest test this place has to offer when you landed. Now, follow me. By the way, miss, just call me Bridge. Lieutenant still sounds a bit pretentious to me."

"OK, Bridge," Trudy said with a bright smile as she followed him up the stairs.

"Now, sir, miss, please pay close attention here 'cause I wasn't jokin' about takin' up half of the floorboards. See here, where we have some board laid out crosswise so that you have a safe path to walk on between the mattresses. These mattresses are laid out across the open boards, and after we did it, we figured out that it makes them a good bit warmer since the heat goes straight into them from below. Just don't get out of the wrong side of the bed, or, as the old saying goes, you will have a very bad day. To wit, we ain't got any doctors here, and we ain't even got a medic. Closest thing we got is one of the privates who helped you tie down. He has a grandpa who's a Cherokee medicine man, and he picked up a few things from him growin' up."

"What about a latrine? I could sure use one now," Trudy said nervously.

"Ain't safe to have an outhouse with the damn bears, so we built one on the ground floor. We keep lye and water in there for you to wash down the shit and keep the smell down, so please use it. You don't want to be here when it gets warm for a couple of days in a row. I learned how to hold my breath longer than a frogman."

Trudy rushed down the stairs to the latrine.

"Bridge, this will be just fine. I see why the general gave you a field promotion. Few men could survive in this environment, let alone thrive and enjoy their job."

"Sir, you do understand. Back home in Alaska, we did the same things that I do every day here, and now I get army pay and free food to boot. That ain't half bad. Now, let's go downstairs and eat, sir."

Trudy and Rod had an amazing meal with more variations on C rations than Rod thought were ever possible. The salmon was some of the best he had ever tasted, and Trudy changed her mind about bear meat after the meal. Rod noticed the lack of alcohol and asked Bridge if he had thought about making a still.

"Sir, it is hard enough keeping these men going without booze, and we never could afford it when I grew up, so I never developed the taste. Ain't no Mormon or nothing, just poor."

"You're probably right about that approach," Rod said as he decided not to break out his flask and offer his hosts a drink.

The sleeping area was as warm as promised. Trudy and Rod slept until first light, and by the time they were dressed, their hosts had already cleared off their airplanes while one of the privates used a truck with a snow blade to clear the runway of drifts. The other private was using a hand crank to top off the fuel tanks of the two Mustangs.

Rod and Trudy ate a breakfast of smoked salmon, canned scrambled eggs, and canned pears from the C rations before bidding farewell and departing the desolate airbase.

"Take care, Bridge," Trudy yelled from the cockpit of her Mustang before yelling the ingrained "Clear!" before starting the engine.

There were no winds to speak of, and the sky was deep blue. As Trudy pushed the throttled forward and leaped into the air, she reflected on a marvelous experience that she would remember for all of her life.

CHAPTER 9
Duxford, England, 18 1525 January 1944

"Trudy, look out over your left wing. We have some company," Rod called out to Trudy over their private channel.

Trudy was a split second from rolling into a dive when she recognized the five aircraft. The planes were approaching from about a thousand feet above their current fifteen-thousand-foot flight path from Liverpool to Duxford, England. She looked up as the Spitfires roared overhead and banked right, flying behind them to join the flight of two Mustangs. Not surprisingly, the Spitfire flight leader had been informed of the Mustang flights' private frequency and made contact.

"Good of you chaps not to shoot us up a bit when we dropped in on you like that. Our ground folks vectored us in. Welcome to England." The Spitfire flight leader spoke in a matter-of-fact tone that was easily detectable even over the radio.

"This is Mustang flight leader. Will you be with us all the way to Duxford?"

"We will at that. That is if we don't need to keep some of the Jerries off your back. I understand that your Mustangs don't have the normal number of stingers, and you might need a bit of help in a pinch."

"That is affirmative. We appreciate that you are riding shotgun for us."

"Right. Well, we should be switching to the Duxford frequency about now. They seem a bit taxed today."

Trudy and Rod both switched to Duxford Tower frequency. They were not yet in sight of the field, so they held off on their first call while they listened to the controllers working hard to sequence damaged fighters returning from escorting bomber raids into Germany. As they got closer to Duxford, there were several P-47 Thunderbolts orbiting the field while firefighters on the ground extinguished the flames of a P-47, which over-ran the runway. Another one of the fighters in the pattern was trailing black smoke from its sputtering engine. Yet another P-47 had a gaping hole in the fuselage and a large section of the vertical stabilizer missing. Trudy and Rod watched in amazement as black smoke from burning aviation fuel from the P-47 at the end of the runway transformed to white smoke and steam as water and foam were used to extinguish the burning plane.

Rod contacted the tower, and both he and Trudy were instructed to enter the pattern and await instructions. The P-47s ahead of them in the pattern were soon on the ground. The Spitfires that had escorted them on the final leg of their journey orbited high above the field, protecting all those below.

Trudy was cleared to land first. She descended as she flew parallel to the runway in her downwind portion of the pattern continuing more than a mile past the end of the runway before making a sharp ninety-degree turn onto the "base" leg of the pattern. As Trudy leveled the Mustang, she could see the end of the runway over her left shoulder as planned. Suddenly, the Mustang lurched nose-up and twisted to the left.

The left wing lost lift, and Trudy immediately recognized the low-speed stall. She pushed the nose down and applied power, and the aircraft was soon performing normally. Trudy noted her speed prior to the stall on her knee board. At 145 mph she had been well above stall speed. This must be one of the "unusual handling characteristics" that Rod had mentioned. As Trudy turned onto final approach, she added a bit more power and noted that at 155 mph the plane seemed to recover from the turn without any problem. Trudy touched down within thirty yards of the end of the runway. She pushed both rudder pedals hard to apply the brakes, felt the main gear shudder, and made the first turn onto the taxiway. Rod was right behind her as she taxied to the ramp in front of the control tower.

Rod and Trudy shut down their planes and quickly unstrapped from their parachutes.

"What happened on the turn onto your base leg? It looked like the left wing stalled," Rod said with a worried look on his face.

"That's what it felt like to me, too. I was at 145 mph, so I should have been well over stall speed," Trudy yelled over the sounds of the Spitfires now making their landings.

"We'll talk inside," Rod said as he headed for base operations.

Less than half an hour later, Rod and Trudy headed into the debriefing room. As the two entered the room, Trudy immediately noticed the stars on one of the four American officers in the room. There was an English army officer standing next to them, but Trudy was unfamiliar with the rank insignia on his shoulder boards.

As Rod and Trudy moved into the room, the American brigadier general moved forward to greet them.

"I'm General Donovan. This is Brigadier Welton from the British Special Operations Executive." General Donovan gestured toward the English officer. "Colonel Campbell, Lieutenant Colonel Stillwater, and Major Kilt work for me, as do you both at the moment, I suppose."

Trudy looked surprised, and it took an awkward second for her to reply. "I am pleased to meet you, sir."

Major Jackson popped into a quick salute, which the general quickly returned, and put out his hand to shake.

"Well done, both of you," Donovan said after shaking both their hands. "You delivered two very expensive planes from halfway around the world. It looked like we almost lost one of them here in Duxford after all that flying. What happened, Miss Andrich?"

"Sir, the left wing stalled at 145 mph, well above normal stall speed for this aircraft. It recovered easily. It did surprise me, though, since this has not happened at that speed anywhere else we landed."

"It is a bit warmer here," Major Kilt said.

"Major Kilt is our aeronautical expert. Major, please continue with any other observations or insights."

"Sir, we have been concerned that the wing modifications to increase the size of the wing tanks may have slightly changed the shape and wing geometry, especially when the wing tanks are near empty. We experienced similar problems on the first hybrid, which Major Jackson flew back in California, but we thought that the problem was fixed during construction of the second and modifications to the first aircraft."

Trudy wondered why Rod had failed to mention the stalling issue specifically, instead just saying that the handling was "quirky."

"So, I was flying the prototype aircraft and Rod, err, Major Jackson was flying the backup," Trudy said with an even more surprised look.

"Well, of course. You have more than three times as many hours in Mustangs as Major Jackson, and you are an experienced test pilot," Major Kilt blurted out.

"Please, everyone sit down," General Donovan instructed as he grabbed a chair for himself.

General Donovan waited for everyone to find their seats before he continued. "Trudy, I noticed how surprised you looked when I mentioned that at least for now you work for me. Let me explain. I authorized the production of these two very specialized airplanes and paid for the logistics associated with getting them halfway around the world because they are vital to accomplish an exceptionally important mission. Until now, you have only been given very general details of that mission, which you have agreed to protect." The general paused as he looked Trudy straight in the eye.

Trudy nodded. "Yes, sir, I did."

The other officers in the room remained silent, recognizing that this was at the moment a private conversation between General Donovan and Trudy.

"Trudy, I know you only signed up to bring me an airplane, but I would like you to consider staying on with us for a few weeks longer and helping us make sure these planes and our pilot are ready for his mission."

"I haven't come all this way just to walk away from an unfinished job, sir. Of course I'll stick around," Trudy said still looking General Donovan straight in the eye.

"I felt certain that you would. I will send a note to Colonel Straight thanking him for choosing the right pilot and authorize him to reveal your status after the mission is complete. As far as everyone will know at the North American plant, those two planes are at the bottom of the Pacific Ocean and were nothing more than a failed experiment."

"Thank you, sir," Trudy replied.

General Donovan now shifted his focus to Major Jackson.

"Major, Brigadier Welton has joined us today to bring us up to date concerning the partisan network that the British have established in Lithuania. I believe you two are acquainted?"

Major Jackson was now the one looking surprised, and he glanced over at the brigadier, almost as if he was looking for permission before he replied. Brigadier Welton gave a slight nod and seemed a bit exasperated at Rod's transparency.

"Yes, sir, I met then Lieutenant Colonel Welton while I was in the hospital in London recovering from wounds that I received at Dieppe."

"It was very kind of him to visit you in the hospital. I'm sure that his visit helped to cheer you up," General Donovan said sarcastically. "Brigadier, please bring us all up to date, and don't spare the details. Miss Andrich will be staying with us until the completion of the mission."

The brigadier stood up, not accustomed to providing a formal briefing while sitting. He paced for a moment as he thought about where to start.

"Thank you, General Donovan. Well, then, as you all know, the special-operations executive has successfully established networks of our agents all across Europe. We strive to expand those networks, and we have been especially effective at recruiting members of the academic community who are particularly offended by Nazi Germany's perversion of science in the pursuit of their totalitarian aspirations. In the Baltic states, Lithuania in particular, we have successfully recruited a scientist who has been conducting research with far-reaching implications. In conversations with this scientist, he has confided that he is working to prove a theory that the differentiation between animal species and the many differentiating traits of species, including man, are the result of a specific biochemical code." The brigadier paused.

"Yes, I know, it sounds like a manufactured story disseminated by atheists to dismiss the role of God. If this information came from one of the many communist-agent networks operating in the Baltics, then I might agree with you. That, however, is not the case. Agent 712 is not only a credible scientist but a very religious Jew."

"Sir, so why hasn't this very religious Jew been sent off to a Nazi concentration camp?" Lieutenant Colonel Stillwater asked.

"A marvelous question, Colonel. We believe it is because the Nazis have come to believe the good doctor's research may be valid, and it also fits well into their dream of creating a master race of humans to rule over the rest of all humanity."

"Perhaps we should just bomb their effort to oblivion and be done with it," Rod said rather emphatically.

"That has been discussed. General Donovan, do you wish to comment at this point?" the brigadier offered.

"Yes, thank you, Brigadier Welton. Major Jackson, your point is well taken, and the brigadier is correct. That strategy has been discussed. I decided against that approach after we did a scientific review of the debriefings of Agent 712, provided by the SOE. Chemists at the Admiralty Research Laboratory and physical scientists working for the British Coal Utilization Research Association all agreed that the assertions of Agent 712 were theoretically possible. Based upon the level of detail Agent 712 provided, we were unable to determine if Agent 712's work had been demonstrated during experiments and work was now focused on confirmation and applications of the work or if the research was strictly theoretical. We were also unable to determine how much of the research was documented and who was aware of or possessed those documents."

"General, I understand that contact must be difficult with Agent 712, but couldn't he answer those questions for us?" Trudy asked.

"He probably could, but Agent 712 understands the importance of his work and our interest. He has informed his contact in SOE that there will be no further discussion other than plans for his safe extraction to Allied or neutral territory. Brigadier, please continue."

"Right, well, yes, there is the rub. We will get no more cooperation from Agent 712 until we agree to extract him and we carry through with that promise. And there is another thing. We believe that the Soviets have also established a very effective partisan network inside German-controlled Lithuania, and they may already be pursuing a strategy to recruit and exfiltrate Agent 712, supporting their own agenda of creating perfect workers and maybe even perfect warriors. General Donovan?" The brigadier looked toward General Donovan for guidance.

"Colonel Campbell, please provide us with the status of the plan to rescue Agent 712." General Donovan gestured with his open right hand toward Colonel Campbell.

"Thank you, sir," Colonel Campbell said as he stood bolt upright in front of his seat without taking a step. "With both aircraft in place here at Duxford, we feel comfortable about conducting some additional flight testing to verify our ability to land these aircraft on an unimproved landing strip and take off safely with an additional passenger. We strongly believe that Miss Andrich should be heavily involved in both the planning process and with that testing due to her previous test-pilot experience."

"Agreed," General Donovan said curtly.

"Sir, we have also discussed with Brigadier Welton the need for more details about his agent network in Lithuania to facilitate our planning and to provide better assurance that we are not simply sending Major Jackson into some elaborate trap designed to disrupt OSS and SOE operations in the Baltics." Colonel Campbell paused.

"Welton, can you make that happen, or do I need to go straight to Downing Street?" General Donovan barked.

"Sir, there are some limits to cooperation even between allies as close as we are, but I will do my best to address Colonel Campbell's concerns."

"Good. Colonel Campbell, please take care of the arrangements for getting Miss Andrich and Major Jackson settled in. I understand that you will be putting them up near the university, with privileges. Make sure to give them a couple of days to get accustomed to the time change and then brief them on all the details concerning the mission. I'm headed back to Washington tomorrow, but I will be in touch. If there are any political problems, contact me immediately. Understood?"

"Yes, sir. Miss Andrich, Major Jackson, please follow me," Colonel Campbell said after saluting General Donovan and heading out the door of the briefing room.

As Colonel Campbell ushered the two pilots out of the briefing room, he bent over and whispered to Trudy.

"I'll be in touch soon."

Trudy nodded and otherwise pretended not to hear. She looked closely at Rod to ensure that he had not picked up on the exchange. Satisfied that Rod had not, she stepped forward to catch up with him.

CHAPTER 10
Cambridge, England, 27 0900 January 1944

Trudy walked down Saint Mary's Street, past the bustling Cambridge market, and saw Rod standing by the front door of Great Saint Mary's Church, just as he had promised. Rod saw her first, and when he was sure that she had seen him, he headed across the street to meet her.

"There is a place for tea just about a block south of here. Are you game?" Rod said.

"That will certainly beat standing out here in the cold. How is your flat?" Trudy asked as she shivered.

"It's nice but small. My feet hang off the end of the bed, but it is clean and well kept.

They headed off and found the place that Rod remembered from a previous visit without any trouble. After being seated in the small but newly remodeled café, they ordered tea. They sat next to the south-facing window, and the morning sun felt warm. A tabby cat was sunning itself on the window sill.

"The cat isn't bothering you, is it?" the waitress asked.

Rod and Trudy both shook their heads no, and Trudy smiled.

"He has the right idea," Trudy commented.

"He is not supposed to be in here, but we don't normally have customers this time of morning. Are you students or from the base?" the waitress inquired.

"From the base," Rod responded.

"Enough said then. Call out if you need anything else."

"She has an unusual accent," Trudy commented after the waitress had disappeared into the back of the shop.

"Yes, slight hint of German or more likely Dutch," Rod said introspectively.

"I assumed that you spoke German, considering what we are involved with. Do you speak Dutch too?" Trudy asked.

"Not Dutch, but with the German I can understand some," Rod replied.

"I would enjoy practicing my German with you, but here in England, that might attract a bit of attention," Trudy laughed.

"Yes, probably wise not to. Any other languages?" Rod asked.

"Yes, Russian, but I'm told I have a Ukrainian accent from my parents. They were first-generation Americans and spoke it fluently and more often than Ukrainian. How about you?"

"Also Russian and some Latin from high school. I also picked up Spanish while I was in Spain," Rod added.

"Spain? When were you there? During the Civil War?" Trudy asked with a slightly puzzled look.

"I spent almost a year there between 1937 and 1938, just before I went to Canada and enlisted," Rod answered.

"I have heard that Spain is a beautiful country, but I have never been there. So you were there during the war. Were you involved somehow?" Trudy asked.

"Yes, but I was mainly involved with aircraft maintenance. I didn't get involved in the actual fighting."

"So you were supporting the Republicans?" Trudy asked.

"Yes. So how is your tea?" Rod said, changing the subject.

"Quite good. Between it and the sun through the window, I am finally warming up for the first time since I left California," Trudy said.

"It is pleasant in here, but I'm afraid that we have some flying to do this afternoon. They said that they would pick us up at the church where I met you, so I guess we had better get going."

Trudy and Rod split the bill and headed off to their rendezvous with their ride to the base. To their surprise there was a young woman with a medic's arm band indicating that she was a member of the ambulance service.

Rod was concerned that they had sent a member of the ambulance service for some other purpose, so he made sure that she was in fact sent to take them to Duxford.

"You were sent here to collect a Major Jackson."

"They actually didn't say who. They just told me to pick up an American man and woman who would be waiting at the church. There is not a lot to do when there are no raids. Thankfully we have had many slow days since the Blitz ended more than a year ago," the young woman commented as they got in. "Did you just get married at the church?"

"No, we are just business associates," Trudy said firmly.

The ride to Duxford was hair raising. The young woman had certainly grown accustomed to dodging obstacles at breakneck speed, and in less than ten minutes, they were waved onto the base at Duxford by sentries at the gate who seemed to know the driver.

CHAPTER 11

Duxford, England, 28 0700 January, 1944

After they were dropped off at base operations, still in their "civvies," both made quick trips to their lockers in the changing rooms to change into their flight suits before they met again in the briefing room. Colonel Campbell was waiting for them.

"Good morning, sir," Rod said as he entered the briefing room with Trudy trailing slightly behind.

"Good morning, Rod, Trudy, please have a seat."

The two pilots were seated, and both took out small notebooks. And when they looked ready to take notes, the colonel stopped pacing and spoke.

"Rod, today we need to make sure that these planes can land safely under the conditions we expect you to encounter in Lithuania. Both aircraft have a light fuel load today, and we don't expect you to be flying for more than ninety minutes or so today. There is a grass strip due west of the base here where you will be attempting some short field landings and takeoffs.

You already know about the tendency to stall, so the trick will be hitting the brakes hard once you are down and hopefully not flipping on your nose. There is a steady ten-knot breeze lined up with the strip, so landing into the wind will help some. There is plenty of space to experiment, so don't try and nail it on the first landing until you have a feel for how the wheels handle the sod. I'll be heading over by jeep with a radio to watch. Our radio frequency is on the board behind me, but keep the chatter to a minimum, since the Nazis are probably listening. Any questions?"

"No, sir," Trudy and Rod answered in turn. They next focused their attention on a young lieutenant who provided them with the weather briefing.

Thirty minutes later, Trudy and Rod were strapping themselves into their Mustangs. It took another ten minutes to go through the startup checklist. Trudy finished first and started her roll to the run-up area before Rod's engine was started. As Trudy executed her S-turns to see the runway in front of her, she saw that Rod was now rolling fast and making an attempt to pass on her right side, perilously close to the edge of the taxiway. Trudy applied the brakes and let him move past her and followed him to the run-up area where she set the brakes and moved the throttle forward as she watched the rpms, left and right magneto, oil pressure, and manifold pressure gauges. Everything looked good, and she gave Rod a thumbs-up, which he returned, and contacted Duxford Tower for permission to take off.

Rod and Trudy took off and climbed to two thousand feet and flew west to the grass strip where they orbited and switched to the frequency that Colonel Campbell had provided.

Trudy maintained her altitude and watched as Rod descended and made a pass over the grass strip at approximately five hundred feet above ground level. He made a mental note that the jeep now parked on the far side of the field had left no tracks when it crossed the grass strip, indicating that the ground was relatively hard. The jeep's occupants had raised a wind sock that indicated that the wind was steady and blowing straight down the runway as they had been briefed.

"It looks fine," Rod said over their private frequency. "Time to show off a little," he said under his breath.

Rod made a second pass over the runway, but instead of entering a parallel pattern, he looped and then rolled level now aiming straight to the runway upwind. Rod slowed to 140 mph before lowering his flaps and then landing gear. As the gear came down, he was almost over the end of the grass strip at less than fifty feet. At ten feet above the runway, Rod cut the engine and let the plane drop like a rock until it made contact with the grass and dirt. The Mustang bounced once very hard. As the plane dropped a second time, it hit first on the outer side of the left gear, which swung the tail of the Mustang faster than Rod could correct it with the rudder since so little air was flowing over the control surfaces at the now very low speed. As the tail swung, the tail gear caught the ground and sheared off. Rod responded by hitting the brakes hard since applying power was now a lost option after he cut the engine. The Mustang flipped nose over onto the propeller. When the propeller hit the ground, it threw sod and dirt in all directions creating a cloud of debris. The aircraft came to rest back on its tail, and with the tail gear now missing, the plane looked like it had sunk into the hard dirt and sod.

Trudy watched in horror as the three occupants of the jeep ran to the plane. She tried to call Rod, but there was no response.

She switched back to the Duxford Tower frequency.

"Mayday, Mayday, Duxford Tower," Trudy called calmly.

"What is the nature of your emergency?" the tower responded.

"Mustang crashed on the grass strip west of Duxford field. Fate of the pilot is unknown," Trudy responded.

Knowing that she could not land on the now damaged grass strip especially with wreckage in the middle of the field, Trudy stayed on the Duxford Tower frequency.

"Duxford Tower, this is Mustang flight minus one, request landing instructions."

Duxford Tower responded routinely, accustomed to aircraft emergencies of all kinds with P-47s routinely operating from the base.

Trudy entered the landing pattern and was on final approach when she received another call from the tower.

"Mustang flight, this is Duxford Tower. I am pleased to pass along that the pilot of the Mustang involved in an incident is unharmed."

Trudy parked the plane and called to have it towed into the hangar before heading to base operations.

"I need a jeep and directions to the grass strip west of here," Trudy said with a sense of urgency to the American sergeant manning the front desk.

"I'll do you one better, Miss. The fire chief is in the loo, and as soon as he comes out, you can ride with him out to the accident site."

As the sergeant finished his sentence, the fire chief emerged from the bathroom, still buttoning his fly.

"Hey chief, this is the wingman, sorry ma'am, of the pilot who trashed his Mustang at the grass strip. Can she ride out there with you?"

"Most certainly, Madam. I was just headed out there when nature called. I hear that your chap is OK, but I'm afraid I can't say that for the airplane. I suppose they'll be expecting me to figure out some way to get it back here. Damn the luck."

"Where is your car?" Trudy said insistently, trying to hurry the long-winded chief.

"Just outside and around back. You don't need a chaperone or some other accommodation before we head out. The loo perhaps," the chief said considerately.

"No, really, I'll be fine. Thank you for the ride," Trudy added.

In less than fifteen minutes, the chief's car was pulling off the paved road onto what looked like a goat path.

"I can't say that I enjoy coming out here," he exclaimed. "This path is meant more for a jeep that this car. Now I'm going to need to send the bloody thing out for a good washing. As you can see, getting a truck out here to retrieve the plane is going to be a bit of a sticky wicket. Of course the drivers can wash their trucks themselves," he added.

As they came over a low rolling hill, they could see the damaged Mustang on the grass strip in front of them. An ambulance was getting ready to leave, and firemen in their bunker gear were standing around the airplane, but there was no sign of a fire. Trudy had noticed on the drive out that there was no sign of smoke and had not expected to see a fire at the crash site.

The chief pulled his car to the opposite side of the fire truck, well away from the Mustang.

"You can't be too careful with the airplanes full of fuel and such. They can flare up at a moment's notice. I've seen it happen many times than I care to remember," the chief droned on.

"Thank you for the ride," Trudy said once more as she bolted out the door of the chief's car as soon as it came to a halt. She ran around the fire truck and headed straight for Colonel Campbell, who was the first person she recognized.

"Sir, is Rod OK?" Trudy asked.

"He is fine for now, but he may not be after General Donovan hears me explain what happened. Did you see what happened from the air, or were you too busy flying?" the colonel said skeptically, expecting her to cover for Rod.

"I saw the whole thing, sir."

"Well, I am glad to hear that. You just sit your ass down in my jeep and start writing down everything you saw before you talk to anyone else. Don't stop writing or sign it until I have a chance to look it over. Got it?"

"Yes, sir," Trudy said compliantly as she headed toward the colonel's jeep.

"How the hell is he going to make it to Lithuania? That is some of the worst flying I have ever seen," Lieutenant Colonel Stillwater exclaimed to the colonel, purposely loud enough for Trudy to hear.

Trudy ignored the comment and kept heading for the jeep. Ignoring it was easy, especially since she agreed with him.

For the next hour, Trudy put the finishing touches on her official statement, then walked over to Colonel Campbell, and handed it to him without saying a word.

The colonel read the three-page statement twice.

"Thank you, Trudy. Go ahead, and sign it. Do you think we can get this bird flying again?" he said as he pointed at the damaged Mustang.

"Sir, they will need a structural engineer to go over it, but it really doesn't look too bad," Trudy said. She was surprised that the colonel was asking her opinion.

The colonel pulled her aside, out of earshot of the others.

"Do you think he did this on purpose?" Colonel Campbell whispered.

"It sure looked like it to me. I think he cut the engine so he would be less likely to burn with the plane, not to show off," Trudy whispered back.

"Yeah. I agree. Be careful, OK?" the colonel whispered.

"Yes, sir," Trudy said out loud. "If the report meets with your expectations, I would like to be dismissed so I can visit Rod at the base infirmary."

"I'll have my driver take you back. I'll be stuck out here until we get this thing moved. Thank you, Miss Andrich." The colonel turned and raised his voice even louder. "Driver, take Miss Andrich back to Duxford."

CHAPTER 12
Cambridge, England, 8 1100 February, 1944

Trudy walked out the door of her quaint Cambridge townhouse into a sunny but damp and cold English day. She kept a regular routine on nonflying days with a brisk walk through the market to explore the Cambridge University campus with a break in the middle to watch the ducks or boats on the River Cam. Today the routine paid off. As Trudy was standing on the bridge looking up the river, admiring the wooden Mathematical Bridge, a well-tanned man about her age and height stopped and stood next to her and seemed to be interested in the wooden bridge too.

"Good morning, Miss Andrich, Colonel Campbell sends his regards," he said with some intermittent glances in her direction as he watched a boat that had also caught Trudy's attention.

"Good morning. Colonel Campbell said that he would be in touch almost two weeks ago. What took so long?"

"SOE is keeping tight tabs on you, and I don't think it is for your protection. They have also made several inquiries about you back in the States. By the way, my name is Captain Richard Ryan, and as far as SOE knows, I don't have any connections with OSS, either, so you are completely safe. If you like, we can pretend to be having a relationship to make future meetings easier," Captain Ryan winked and smiled during another quick glance toward Trudy.

"I thought you said that I was completely safe? So what did Colonel Campbell send you here to tell me?" Trudy said turning toward Captain Ryan and posing a bit flirtatiously.

"SOE has several reasons for not wanting this mission to go ahead. We think that some of their network in Lithuania are doubles, also working for the Russians. They want them in place when the Russians eventually take back Lithuania from the Nazis, which we expect will happen in a few months."

"That explains some of the bad decisions and accidents. Rod put one of the planes out of commission for over a week with a hard landing practicing on a dirt runway. Bringing the planes over in the middle of winter was asking for trouble too. But why go to all that trouble? If Rod is working for them or someone else, all he needs to do is screw up the mission?"

"His intent is not to scrub the mission. We think that he intends to kill the professor, not rescue him. He may be suspicious that the second plane is more than a backup, and he wants to make sure that he is alone on the mission. We just aren't sure if it is he alone or SOE that wants to make sure the backup plane is not available," Captain Ryan said as he surveyed Trudy's figure on his next glance in her direction.

"What difference will that make?"

"Because General Donovan has intended all along to send you also. The professor has a wife who he wants out too, or he may not be coming along."

"Is she worth saving, or is it just sentimental?"

"She may be one of the SOE principals who set this in motion, but the SOE will never admit that to us.

Colonel Campbell will brief everyone on the mission change when you get together next week for the formal mission briefing."

"Why don't the SOE have their network in place to kill the professor and be done with it?"

"Even the SOE boys are worried about the professor falling into the hands of the Russians. Their doubles might just sell him to the NKVD for a higher price if they were put up to killing him."

"That makes sense. Now turn toward me, and shake hands. Then ask for my number."

"I will, but I already have your number. Can I call you about getting together next Friday?"

"For another message from Colonel Campbell?" Trudy looked at Captain Ryan skeptically.

"No, just to keep up appearances and to get to know each other better."

"I think I prefer that we meet like this a few more times, and we'll see how it goes," Trudy said coyly.

"OK, but we don't have a lot of time. I know the new schedule," Captain Ryan said with a smart aleck grin, before he turned to head off in the opposite direction from where Trudy would go to head back home.

Trudy smiled and watched Captain Ryan head off and glanced around before she headed back home. There was an older man in a tweed hat and jacket sitting on a bench nearby who seemed to be interested in her, but that might not have anything to do with surveillance, Trudy thought as she stepped into a brisk pace. As she did, the man in tweed folded his newspaper and got up to follow her. "I hope the old fart is in good shape," Trudy said under her breath as she picked up the pace a bit more and took the long way back to her flat.

CHAPTER 13

Duxford, England,
15 0900 February, 1944

Trudy headed into the briefing room and took a seat next to Rod. All the seats in the front rows were full already, but Rod had saved a seat for her. There was an air of nervousness, with some in attendance staying completely silent while they waited and others talking or joking a little bit too loud.

"Good morning, Trudy. You seem to be running a little bit late. I don't normally beat you into the briefing room. I thought Colonel Campbell would start without you, but he also seems to be a few minutes late. Everything OK?" Rod inquired.

"Yes, I just had a late night."

"Out with that army captain again, I'll bet. Don't get too attached to him. They'll just be shipping him off somewhere before you know it," Rod said slyly.

"So I guess you thought that I would be better off going out with you instead?"

"Of course. At least you know when I'm going and when I'll be back. Since I'm a pilot, I can even find some reason to fly back to California and visit you," Rod said with an evil smile.

"I don't think you will need to go all that way on my account, but it will always be nice to see you occasionally, because of all the travels we have had together," Trudy said with a smile, but keeping her eyes fixed on Colonel Campbell who was headed toward the podium. *I wonder if this will be the day he breaks the news to them,* she thought.

"Aten hut!" Lieutenant Colonel Stillwater yelled out as Colonel Campbell approached the podium next to the stage.

Colonel Campbell nodded toward a young sergeant standing next to the curtains at the front of the room. The sergeant pulled on the cords, and the curtains were opened to reveal the map of Europe, which showed flight routes originating at Duxford and heading to Berlin and then Kaunas, Lithuania.

"Good morning, everyone. Take your seats. As you might have gathered by the size of the audience today, this will be our formal mission briefing. First I would like to get something out of the way. There has been a major change in our plan that I need to brief you about. Instead of only sending Rod, we are going to be sending both Mustangs. And just before the meeting, I spoke with Trudy, and she has agreed to pilot the other Mustang all the way to Lithuania and back."

Rod looked horrified.

"That's ridiculous, sir. Trudy doesn't have the training required for this mission," Rod said loudly.

"Major, you don't interrupt me. Now shut up, and let me get through this briefing. You'll have a chance to ask questions when I am through," Colonel Campbell said sharply as he pointed at Rod.

"Yes, sir," Rod said with a slight air of disrespect.

Colonel Campbell continued. "First I would like to introduce Colonel Eschelman, commander of the 447th Bomber Group at Rattlesden, England. The 447th's bombing mission will be the cover for our penetration into German airs pace. We originally planned to accompany a bombing mission to Berlin, but the losses we have been taking have delayed the Berlin daylight missions until March. Every day we spend here on the ground, the Russians are pushing the Germans back and getting closer to our target. As it turns out, Berlin would have taken us farther out of our way than required too. Instead of Berlin, Trudy and Rod will accompany the 447th to a target in the vicinity of Rostock, along the Baltic coast. When the 447th hits their targets, Trudy and Rod will descend below German radar and head across the Baltic to the Lithuanian coast. Colonel Eschelman, do you have anything to add?"

Colonel Eschelman stood up and turned toward Rod and Trudy.

"I want to assure you both that the final destination of your mission will not be known to the rest of my men. Colonel Campbell's people have already spread rumors via some bar talk that we will have some additional company to test out the ability of the new P-51D to escort us closer to our targets. We took this precaution in case any of my men are shot down and captured. We can't be sure what they would say under torture. Lastly, thank you both for your bravery. General Donovan personally called to ask for my squadron's cooperation, and he explained to me just how important this mission is. God bless you both," Colonel Eschelman said as he returned to his seat.

"Thank you, Colonel Eschelman. I would also like to introduce Colonel Spicer, commander of the 357th Fighter Group in Leiston, England. The 357th is currently flying P-51Bs, and they are slated to get the P-51D in late summer, so your P-51Ds won't stick out like a sore thumb when you follow them in on the escort mission. Colonel Spicer's men have all been told that this is a test of the new plane that they will be getting. His men will be escorting you both and keeping you just as safe as the bombers. Also, Rod, Trudy, they don't need your help with any German fighters. Especially since you have had most of your Brownings removed, don't try and mix it up with any Nazi planes that get through. Clear?"

Trudy and Rod both answered with a simultaneous "Yes, sir."

"Colonel Spicer, do you have anything to add?" Colonel Campbell asked as he gestured toward Colonel Spicer.

"We will take good care of your people and the bombers, Colonel," Colonel Spicer said as he remained seated, choosing not to acknowledge Trudy or Rod.

"Thank you, Colonel Spicer. Lastly, I would like to introduce Squadron Commander Balwin of the 156th Squadron, Group 8, Path Finder Force. Squadron Commander Balwin is slated to provide twenty of his Lancasters that have been specially equipped with the best navigation equipment that we can produce. The 156th has developed this capability to lead the many night missions into Germany, allowing the Brits to more accurately bomb at night while we bomb during the day. The 156th is stationed at Upwood, northwest of us. They will be over Rattlesden when the 447th starts taking off in their B-17s. The 156th was brought in because this time a year the Baltic coast is often socked in with clouds, and even during daylight, navigation may be difficult. Squadron commander, welcome. Do you have anything to add?"

"Don't mind if I do. Honored to be pulled into a party like this. I wanted to assure you that we will know the way. Tonight, twenty of my specially equipped Lancasters will be leading a force of 561 bombers right over Rostock, continuing south to Berlin on a night raid, where we plan to drop more than twelve hundred tons of high explosive and fourteen hundred tons of incendiary bombs on the Jerries. We will adjust the route that we take you to Rostock, based on what we encounter tonight. Now I am afraid that you must excuse me since my squadron is flying tonight, and it will be briefing time before we know it," the squadron commander said as he paused in front of Rod and Trudy before hurrying out of the room, unable to find appropriate words of encouragement in this new setting.

"Thank you, Squadron Commander," Colonel Campbell said. "Our detailed flight briefings will be at 0500 on the morning of the twentieth at each of our respective bases. Are there any questions, Rod?"

Rod had drifted away for a moment back to Blue Beach, on the shores of the village of Puys less than two kilometers east of Dieppe. Artillery fire was raining down, and it was so hard running through the sand with his sergeant's limp body draped across his back.

"Major Jackson, now is the time," Colonel Campbell prompted him once more.

"Yes, sir. Miss Andrich is not trained for what we will face when we get on the ground. Our mission inside Lithuania is even more complex than the plan to get us there."

"Major Jackson, we will discuss this in depth when we meet with you both in a smaller setting to go over what happens on the ground. Your reservations are noted, but from what I have seen, she has a better shot at getting to the target in one piece than you do," Colonel Campbell said. "Trudy, how about you? Any questions?"

Trudy felt good about the public support and confidence that the colonel had just demonstrated, and she hesitated a moment before asking a question while the colonel waited.

"Sir, what sort of defenses can we expect along the Lithuanian coast?"

"Good question, Trudy. We have very limited intelligence, but it doesn't seem to be heavily defended. The RAF has bombed Konigsberg in Prussia at night, but we have never ventured that far on daylight bombing missions, and the few OSS insertions that we have made were all at night with parachute drops and no landings. If you are seen by someone on the ground, you will likely be mistaken for one of the more than forty-seven hundred P-39 Air Cobras or two thousand–plus P-63 King Cobras that we have given the Russians under the Lend Lease program. Since you will be heading east, they will probably just think that you are hightailing it back to Russian air space after a recon mission. If you do run into German aircraft at that point, either outrun them or use the two Browning .50 cals that you each still have to shoot them down as a last resort."

"What about the landing site? That hasn't even been mentioned," Rod said impatiently.

"Rod, you and Trudy will be briefed on the landing site and how to link up with the partisans the day after tomorrow in London. The three of us will be traveling by car tomorrow for a meeting with General Eisenhower late that afternoon, and then on Thursday we will spend the entire day at the SOE Baker Street headquarters."

"So, that's why they call them the Baker Street Irregulars," Trudy said as she made the connection for the first time.

"Yes, and they also jokingly refer to themselves as the Department of Ungentlemanly Warfare, so watch yourself around those fellows," Rod said as he winked at Trudy.

"I imagine that we will be dining with SOE Thursday night, so pack for three days. My driver will pick you up at your flats in Cambridge tomorrow at 0700. I will be going on ahead with Lieutenant Colonel Stillwater, and we will meet for lunch after you get settled in temporary quarters," Colonel Campbell instructed.

Trudy and Rod provided the required "Yes, sir" to Colonel Campbell as the colonel turned and departed.

"Well, this should be fun. I hope you know what you have gotten yourself into," Rod said sarcastically to Trudy.

Trudy just smiled at the comment while thinking about her opportunity to finally apply some of the OSS training that she had only practiced.

The briefing room emptied quickly.

CHAPTER 14

London, England, 16 1200 February 1944

"**S**o, where are we headed now?" Trudy inquired as she sat in the back seat of Colonel Campbell's sedan with Rod.

"I was instructed to follow directions to the Whitfield Memorial Church on Tottenham Court Road. Colonel Campbell said that we would recognize the place as soon as we arrived. It's some kind of bunker, I believe. The colonel said that he would meet us inside," Colonel Campbell's driver remarked.

"We just passed Baker Street. It's convenient for SOE that they are so close to Ike's HQ," Rod chimed in after drifting off into a waking dream again for a few moments.

"The repair work around here is amazing. I am stunned at how fast they have cleared out rubble from all the bombings and rebuilt," Trudy commented as the driver maneuvered around a pile of bricks that partially blocked the road.

"Yes, it is really quite amazing. A true example of keeping a stiff upper lip and pushing on, as they say around here," Rod replied.

"There is the church. That brick building. It says Whitfield Memorial Church above the double doors in front," Trudy pointed out.

"Look off to your right. The colonel wasn't kidding about recognizing the headquarters. It looks like a bloody fortress," Rod exclaimed.

The driver stopped the car next to the curb.

"You can get out here. I'll find a place to park and wait in the car," the driver offered.

"OK, but who knows how long we will be. These flag-ranked officers seem to ignore their schedules, and they never start on time for folks like us," Rod said sarcastically.

Across the street from the church, Trudy and Rod paused to look at the round pillbox-style bunker with a blockhouse on top that looked several stories tall and another angular bunker almost as tall off to their right. Between the two structures was a one-story structure with a steel door in the middle. Military sentries were posted in front of the door, and the barrels of heavy machine guns could be seen extending from the slits in the square bunker to their left.

Trudy and Rod approached the sentries and were just about to introduce themselves to the guard who appeared to be in charge when Colonel Campbell stepped out to greet them.

"They saw you drive up and phoned inside that you had arrived. Welcome to General Eisenhower's headquarters in Europe," Colonel Campbell said with a broad smile. He seemed genuinely excited.

Colonel Campbell led them past three levels of tight security to a narrow stairway that descended steeply underground. There was a landing more than two stories underground, and then the stairs went two more stories underground in the opposite direction. At the very bottom of the stairs, two burly-looking American MPs holding Thompson submachine guns, in addition to Colt .45 pistols on their belts, looked over the three visitors and waved them through another steel door. Inside the last door, the interior was brightly lit, which was especially noticeable as they left the dim lighting of the stairwell. A long hallway with offices on each side stretched for at least fifty feet. Colonel Campbell walked down the middle of the hallway leading Rod and Trudy to the last office. Inside, there was an elegantly dressed English woman at a desk next to an inner office door. Off to the side was another desk with an attractive uniformed member of the Woman's Army Corps typing briskly as she looked up and smiled at Rod.

"Please have a seat. The general will be ready for you in no time at all," the English secretary said in a very proper upper-class accent.

Colonel Campbell pointed at the new leather couch along the other wall and instructed Rod and Trudy to sit while he sat down in a comfortable-looking overstuffed leather chair that faced slightly toward the couch.

"Remember what I said in the car, Trudy. We'll be sitting out here for hours," Rod whispered to Trudy loudly enough for everyone in the room to hear above the typing.

As if on cue, a buzzer went off at the English secretary's desk. "The general will see you now," she said with a frown focused on Rod.

Colonel Campbell gave a nod of encouragement and a brief smile as he led the way to General Eisenhower's office. He was just about to knock when the general surprised him by opening the door. General Eisenhower smiled.

"Please come in, and sit down. Major Jackson, Miss Andrich, please sit down over there so we can chat for a few minutes," the general said as he sat down at a small conference table with them instead of taking a seat behind his desk.

"Miss Andrich, Colonel Campbell was explaining to me before you got here that you are one of the first women recruited into the OSS and the very first woman pilot in General Donovan's organization. General Donovan also described to me the nature of your mission during our trip from Washington at the beginning of the month. I want you to know that General Donovan assured me that not only you are a superb pilot, but your OSS training scores were better than many of the male recruits, especially your combatives and shooting skills."

Rod looked stunned at first and then embarrassed as the general shifted his focus to him.

"Rod, I believe that you are the first American to receive the Victoria Cross in this war. I read about your heroics at Dieppe. Well done, Major. As you may know, I have never served in combat. I especially admire all of you who have. The mission that you are about to lead will have grave consequences for humanity if you fail. I don't fully understand the science behind it, but President Roosevelt's most senior scientific advisers have emphasized the importance of the scientist you are being sent to rescue. I want you to know that I have full confidence in you both, and Colonel Campbell has my authority to get you anything you need for success. Do you understand, Colonel Campbell?" the general said as he turned to look at the colonel.

"Yes, sir," Colonel Campbell said curtly.

"Very well, then. Best of luck to you both. I understand that you will be spending the day with the SOE, and Colin has assured me that you will get their fullest cooperation," General Eisenhower said as he stood up and held out his hand to shake hands with Trudy. Rod popped a quick salute, which he held until the general returned it and turned to retreat behind his desk, which was their cue to leave.

Colonel Campbell guided Trudy and Rod out of the general's office and closed the door behind them as they departed.

"So, who is Colin?" Trudy asked Rod in a hushed voice.

"Major General Colin Gubbins, the director of SOE," Rod replied. "So, when were you going to tell me that you were trained for this mission?" Rod said with an exasperated look on his face.

"When I was sure that I would be going. When were you going to tell me that you were a hero at Dieppe?" Trudy replied.

"Everyone was a hero at Dieppe. In spite of it being a disaster," Rod said as they walked down the hallway and past the MP to the stairwell.

"So, what now?" Trudy asked as they started the climb up the four long flights of stairs.

"I don't know about you, but tonight I'm going to Piccadilly Circus. You are welcome to come along."

"As your date, or otherwise?"

"I would be delighted if you would come as my date, but I'm guessing you would prefer to join me as a fellow comrade in arms. Am I right?"

"You are, and who knows, we might both get lucky tonight," Trudy said, only half joking.

"Eight o'clock in the lobby then?"

"Eight o'clock it is," Trudy agreed.

"Who knows, maybe we will see Winston Churchill. I hear that he eats at the Savoy frequently," Rod commented.

"Well, we just had a private meeting with the supreme commander of Allied Forces in Europe, so why would you be surprised?" Trudy laughed.

CHAPTER 15
London, England,
17 0800 February 1944

Rod climbed into the back of the cab waiting for them at the front of the Savoy Hotel and scooted over so that Trudy could get in more easily.

"Sixty-four Baker Street," Rod barked at the cabdriver.

"So, what time did you get in last night?" Trudy teased when she noticed Rod rubbing his eyes and forehead.

"Probably before you. Those English women pilots you introduced me to were absolutely insane," Rod said as he continued to rub his forehead. "What are they called over here, Women Auxiliary Air Force?"

"Yes, but the girls I introduced you to are pilots, and the Women's Auxiliary Air Force is limited to support functions. The girls we partied with were Air Transport Auxiliary. The ATA are civilian pilots in uniform just like the WASPs back home," Trudy said proudly.

"My god, how those women could drink. I think they were trying to take advantage of me."

"By the looks of you, they did," Trudy joked.

"Here we are, then," the cabdriver interrupted as he pulled up to the curb.

Rod paid the fare and waited for Trudy to get out curbside before he exited on the same side.

There was a surprising lack of obvious security at the SOE headquarters. A single bobby stood outside the door.

"Good morning. I believe they are expecting you two," was all that he said as he pointed toward the door up the steps.

Rod knocked on the door, and a bespectacled young man a head shorter than Rod opened the door and motioned them inside.

"Good morning, I'm Major Jackson, and this—"

"Please, don't say another word, and follow me," the young man said as he led them into the library.

"We really don't need to go through all of this. I have been here before," Rod said with an exasperated tone.

"Well, you have not been where I'm about to take you. So you will please do me the courtesy of behaving like a guest and shut your mouth for the time being. Miss Andrich has caught on, hasn't said a word, and I know it is not because she is timid."

Rod rolled his eyes as the young man pushed on the bookcase, which opened a doorway that led to a steep staircase.

"Please follow me," the young man said as he led the way down the stairs into an old basement. On the opposite side of the basement from the stair landing was a lit passageway that appeared to have been hewn out of solid rock. The young man led the way into the passage, which was about seven feet tall and barely wide enough for two people to pass.

"Watch your head on the lights, Major. You are a tall fellow, after all," the young man said as he neared the end of the underground passage and unlocked a steel blast door that opened into another residential basement.

Trudy and Rod followed the young man up the stairs into another elaborately decorated townhome. The art on the walls was literally price-less, and the leather furniture was plush and well worn. They continued through several rooms and headed to the back door. There was a covered walkway out the backdoor that led to a Rolls-Royce in the alleyway with an open passenger door. The young man continued to lead Trudy and Rod to the waiting car and helped them both in before he opened the front door and climbed in next to the driver.

When he closed the door of the car, his demeanor immediately changed, and the pleasant smile he had maintained disappeared.

"That was bloody stupid taking a taxi here from the Savoy Hotel. That place is normally full of journalists. But then it is stupidity like that that has caused us to take these elaborate security measures. I am Colonel Nigel Scott, SOE, and I am pleased to make your acquaintance," he said before giving the driver a nod to proceed.

"We didn't have much of a choice about using the cab. Colonel Campbell is using his car today and left us without transportation," Trudy explained.

"Well, that's bloody resourceful of you. I do not suppose you could have taken a cab someplace close and walked a bit? Maybe on such a bright morning the sun would have affected your complexion?" Colonel Scott said with thick sarcasm.

Trudy realized this was not a winnable battle, and she bit her lip and remained silent. She nudged Rod, intending to keep his mouth shut, but it was too late.

"Not much in the way of security at your headquarters, is there, Colonel?" Rod chimed in as a dig.

"The bobby standing outside is simply there to warn off solicitors and the lost or drunken American GIs who might stumble down the street. You were covered with several machine guns and a sniper or two as soon as you turned onto the block. You must realize that we are not new at this. We have been fighting the IRA here at home for some time now."

"Colonel, where are we going?" Trudy asked as the Rolls-Royce maneuvered through the city at breakneck speed.

"Finally, an intelligent question, and once again, I am not too surprised it is from you," the colonel responded in an attempt to instigate another outburst from Rod.

Rod remained silent and stared straight back with his steely blue eyes at the colonel, nearly expressionless.

"Well. You two might do, after all," the colonel exclaimed in Russian.

"I believe it is your job to make sure that we succeed," Trudy responded in perfect German.

The colonel smiled again.

"Right, then. Well played. Now, enough of this butt sniffing like dogs meeting for the first time. Please be so kind, and let me get on with the business at hand," the driver said, as he spoke for the first time.

"Yes, sir. Major Jackson, Miss Andrich, please let me introduce Major General Gubbins, commander, Special Operations Executive."

"Well, thank you both for putting up with this elaborate escapade. We assume that the Germans have bugged our advertised headquarters or will eventually, so we take special precautions with missions like yours. We are headed out of town to one of the estates that SOE borrows from time to time. Everyone who you need to speak with will be there. We have already sent for your things at the hotel. We will give your bags a bit of a going over, and then they will be placed in your rooms at the estate where we hope that you will agree to dine with us tonight before we send you back to Cambridge in the morning. Will that be satisfactory?" General Gubbins asked sincerely.

Trudy and Rod quickly agreed.

"I guess your driver has the day off today, General," Rod said out of curiosity.

"Actually, he is following in my official sedan. I rather enjoy driving my Rolls, and I thought it might be a treat for you both to go for a drive in the English countryside riding in it. Especially considering that you flew halfway around the world already in Rolls-Royce–powered contraptions."

"The only thing better would be driving it," Trudy said jokingly.

Without warning, the general pulled off to the side of the road.

"Nigel, get in back with the major. Miss Andrich, please get behind the wheel, as a favor, while I provide directions."

Rod chuckled as Trudy exited the car and got into the driver's seat while the colonel, who was not amused, moved into the back seat with Rod. The general, beaming with pride, got into the front passenger seat.

"There now, Miss Andrich, I did promise Ike that I would provide you with anything you asked for. I hope that this is a good start. Let's be off, then. We have about another hour to go before we reach the estate."

Trudy restarted the car and entered the highway, careful to obey the speed limit while driving what was obviously the general's pride and joy.

"Come now, it will be two hours instead of one at this pace. I can assure you that you won't get pulled over in this car," the general said in a jolly tone.

Trudy didn't need very much encouragement, and she accelerated rapidly, pushing everyone back in their seats for a moment. The car rode as if it was hovering above the road and yet still on the curvy highway; it responded to the steering wheel as efficiently as Trudy's Mustang did to the stick.

"This is a real pleasure to drive, General," Trudy said, as she sped down the two-lane road at more than eighty miles per hour.

CHAPTER 16
Wiltshire, England,
17 1020 February 1944

ollowing the general's directions, Trudy arrived at the estate ahead of schedule and pulled into the circular driveway out front. Rod and Colonel Scott had remained uncharacteristically quiet throughout the trip, and Trudy guessed that the drive had them both a bit carsick. Trudy suddenly smiled as she thought about how hard Rod and the colonel had likely held back any event that would have soiled the general's beautiful car.

"Well, you seem to have enjoyed that," Rod said as he noted the smile on Trudy's face as he exited the car.

"In more ways than you know." Trudy smiled back.

"You two look a little bit worse for wear. Are you sure that you fly airplanes, Major? It was only a forty-five-minute ride, after all," the general teased as he headed to the front door of the estate.

At the front door, a butler opened the door as they neared, and he greeted the general.

"Sir, your other guests are gathered for tea in the parlor to the left."

The general led the way to the formal parlor and moved around the room to greet the mix of military and formally dressed civilians. Tea was served, and all the other guests introduced themselves individually to Trudy and Rod. After about thirty minutes, the butler rang a handbell, and the group moved into the formal dining room. Inside, they started seating themselves without further prompting. Colonel Scott pulled a chair away from the table to seat Trudy between him and the general at the head of the table. Major Jackson sat across from Trudy. A projection screen was attached to the wall opposite the general, and Trudy could see that heavy velvet curtains had been retracted and probably hid the screen from view most of the time. A slide projector was in the center of the table, and a British army captain sitting next to the projector turned it on. With a flick of the controls, a man's face appeared on the screen. He looked like he was in his late thirties, with thinning black hair and strong masculine features softened by his round wire-rimmed glasses.

Colonel Scott got up and moved to the front of the room next to the screen. The butler reappeared and handed the colonel a five-foot-long wooden pointer.

"Good morning, General Gubbins, officers, guests. Thank you for gathering with us today. I trust that everyone has had a chance for introductions?" The colonel paused as heads nodded, and those gathered glanced around the table to make sure that there was not some parlor trick afoot.

"Very good. Let us get started. The man you see on the screen is Professor Samuel Michalonis. The professor has degrees in both physical science and biology. With this unique combination of skills, he has broken new ground in the understanding of not only what differentiates man from beast but what differentiates one human from another. The Nazis have, of course, become interested in his work as they seek to create what they believe will be a master race of human hybrids."

"Ghastly," the general interrupted and then nodded for the colonel to proceed.

"To complicate matters, Professor Michalonis is Jewish and thus is not trusted by the Nazis. He is free to move about the city of Kaunas to visit associates and go about his work, but if he attempts to leave the city, he will be arrested. Our underground sources have confirmed the twenty-four-hour-per-day surveillance. Next slide, please. Getting into the city is also difficult. Kaunas, as you can see on the screen, is the shape of a triangle, with rivers on the north and south sides of the city intersecting at the west, where the university is located. The Gestapo have checkpoints established on all the bridges and the highways leading to the city from the east."

"What about the local population, sir?" Rod asked.

"The local government is complicit with the Nazis. Similar to the Vichy in France, they keep their positions and property in return for their cooperation. Fortunately for us, most of the local population does not care one way or the other who is in control, and yet another, although smaller, faction supports a substantial underground resistance movement. Next slide, please."

The screen in front now showed a heavy man in his early thirties with short, curly black hair.

"The man you see in front of you now is Jonas Necris. Mr. Necris is one of our top SOE agents in Lithuania. Necris is a Palestinian Jew born to Lithuanian parents who left Lithuania just prior to the German invasion of Russia. He volunteered for SOE as did a number of other Jews from Palestine who are now working for us across Eastern Europe. Necris was twelve years old at the end of the Great War. He grew up in Ezerelis, just west of Kaunas. Ezerelis is in a heavily forested region of the country. Thankfully, many Lithuanian Jews fleeing from the Nazis have joined the resistance and hidden out in this rural region. Are there any questions at this point?" Colonel Scott paused.

"Sir, I was told that some of the partisans may have sympathy for the communists. Can Necris be trusted?" Trudy asked.

"Necris has been thoroughly vetted, and we are as certain as can be about his loyalty to the Crown, but he has confirmed to us that some of his group members are already feathering their own nests by cooperating with the Russians. It is fairly obvious to most that the Germans will soon be pushed out of Lithuania and the Russians will be in charge. In the same manner that we inserted Necris, the NKVD has been inserting their own people, and they are having a much easier time of it. Proximity and all."

"So, if we land in territory controlled by these partisans of mixed loyalties, how can we be sure that our planes will be there when we get back?" Trudy asked with a frown.

"Captain, move ahead to the flight map. Thank you. Yes, well, Necris has arranged to construct a runway on his family's peat farm. They already have the heavy equipment for the farming. The Nazis haven't shown much interest in the peat farm, either. To get to your landing site, you will follow the Neman River from the coast almost due east. As you can see at this little town, Vilkija, the river takes a sharp bend south, which you will follow at a heading of one hundred eighty degrees, and you will fly over the small town in front of you, which will be Ezerlis. South of Ezerlis is a series of small ponds used to drain the peat fields. Less than one mile west of those ponds will be a line of peat fires. Your landing strip will be parallel to those fires less than fifty meters to the west. It may be nearly dark by the time you get to your target, so the fires will provide an extra margin of safety if you do arrive after sunset. In any case, the darkness will also allow your planes to be moved into a nearby barn."

"So, how do we get to Kaunas and back?" Rod asked.

"We plan to have you taken by car to Akedemija, where we have a safe house. That will get you past the first bridge across the Neman, which is heavily guarded. In Akedemija you will be taken by boat approximately two kilometers upriver to Kaunas, where you will disembark at Santkos Park, which will allow you to move onto the university grounds without too much suspicion. We are told that it is common for coeds to sneak into the park for midnight dalliances."

"So, why do we need to go to the university at all? Why can't the partisans bring the professor to us?" Trudy inquired.

"Excellent question. That would be the best course of action, and we have suggested it. The professor, however, does not trust the partisans not to turn him over to the Russians. As a Lithuanian, he finds the Russians even more distasteful than the Germans. Lithuanians hold Americans in quite high regard, and he will trust you both to secure his freedom. Any further questions before we break for lunch? After lunch we will have experts go over more photographs and more detailed maps of the area."

Trudy and Rod both shook their heads, indicating that there were no more questions at the moment.

"Lunch sounds good. I am famished," Trudy said as she stood up.

The general came to his feet and spoke.

"Very good, all. So for the next few moments, we will retire to the parlor for drinks while they prepare this room for lunch. The facilities are down the hallway past the parlor. Trudy, you are welcome to use the loo at the top of the stairs. It is a bit more private."

With that, the group returned to the parlor with several officers going outdoors to smoke while others took turns going in and out of the loo. Drinks were served at the bar by a steward Trudy had not noticed before.

In almost exactly one half hour, the butler rang the handbell once more, and the group headed back into the dining room. The room had been transformed with drapes pulled to hide the projector screen, white linen tablecloths adorning the dining table, and silver chafing dishes on side tables along the wall. The plates were set with Wedgwood china and crested silverware.

Colonel Scott once again attended to Trudy's chair as everyone returned to their original seats. Meanwhile, footmen from the kitchen delivered plated roast beef, potatoes, and squash. Bottles of claret were also delivered, and glasses were filled.

"This squash is amazingly fresh. We do not normally get any this time of year in Connecticut," Trudy complimented the general.

"We have both an orangery and a large greenhouse out back, so we are getting spring squash earlier than most," the general said proudly.

"Yes, and the beef is quite good today, too," Colonel Scott added.

Lunch and small talk went on for an hour and a half, and Rod grew impatient that the mission was not discussed at all during the meal. Trudy was more accustomed to the informal break, having watched her father get to know his clients in these settings to make the business discussions that followed easier.

After lunch the room was again cleared, and Rod and Trudy were provided with hundreds of photos that showed maps, local Gestapo, university professors, and even discussions of prevailing weather patterns in the local area. By late afternoon the group was rejoined by the general, who had been taking care of other business in another room of the estate.

"I trust this has been a productive afternoon?" the general asked Trudy and Rod.

With all eyes focused on them, Rod responded first.

"Yes, sir, it has," Rod replied.

"Your staff has agreed to contact us with any updates they receive prior to the twentieth, when we depart. They have been extremely thorough and courteous," Trudy added.

"Very good. Now I expect everyone needs a couple of hours to unwind and get changed for dinner, so dinner will be in this room at seven, with cocktails in the parlor starting at six. I look forward to seeing you all then," the general concluded before exiting out the door behind his chair.

Tired from the virtual firehose flow of information they had just received, Trudy and Rod retired to their rooms upstairs for a few moments of quiet.

Trudy used the spare half hour before she needed to change to practice twenty minutes of yoga to stretch after a day of sitting down and for the calm that she needed after the hurried day.

Rod also went straight to his room and soon dozed off, lying on top of the bed with his uniform on except for the jacket. Soon Rod was back on that beach again.

Lieutenant Roderick Jackson, with troops of the Royal Regiment of Canada and the Black Watch (Royal Highland Regiment) of Canada, landed late through no fault of their own. The enemy artillery and machine guns guarding the Dieppe beaches fired at them relentlessly. The same big guns that they had sent to take out by surprise were pinning them down on the beach.

"We will never make it out of here alive," Rod said out loud as he woke up in a cold sweat.

Rod grabbed a flask from his uniform jacket pocket and took a quick swig.

"Time to get ready for dinner, I guess," he said out loud.

Rod arrived at the parlor, clean and wearing a fresh uniform at 6:00 p.m. on the dot. There were already two of the captains and a civilian who had briefed them that afternoon chatting with drinks in hand. Rod quickly acquired a bourbon, neat.

At ten minutes after six, Trudy came down the stairs to join the party gathering in the parlor. She was halfway down the stairs, slowed by three-inch heels, when Colonel Campbell and Lieutenant Colonel Stillwater arrived at the front door. Stillwater's mouth dropped open for a second as he stopped and stared at the beautiful blond woman coming down the stairs in a formal black-silk cocktail dress. Colonel Campbell gave a quick wave.

"Good evening, Miss Andrich," Colonel Campbell said as he hurried into the parlor to keep from staring as Trudy continued down the stairs.

Lieutenant Colonel Stillwater waited for Trudy at the bottom of the stairs.

Trudy stepped forward to greet the lieutenant colonel, standing eye to eye with him in her high heels.

"Colonel, I didn't expect to see you or Colonel Campbell here tonight," she said with a smile.

"Please, Miss Andrich, call me Allen," Lieutenant Colonel Stillwater said as he was suddenly amazed at how light blue Trudy's eyes were.

"Allen it is, but you need to call me Trudy."

"Trudy, it is then, too."

"So, as I was saying, I didn't expect to see you here tonight. What is it that you do for Colonel Campbell?" Trudy asked coyly.

"I am the chief of counterintelligence for our group at Duxford, which is why we need to talk. Can you step into the library with me for a moment?"

"Of course, but maybe you should pick up a book and hold it with both hands in case someone comes in. That would be a counterintelligence kind of thing, wouldn't it?"

"It might be less suspicious if an intruder thought we were philandering, but I will indulge you if it makes you feel safer," Allen said.

Allen led the way into the library and pulled the first book off the shelf that he could reach.

"Trudy, I have some concerns about your partner. We have information that leads us to believe he is working for another government besides ours. Does that surprise you?"

"No, not at all. Others have hinted that he may be working for SOE. It is fairly likely that they recruited him while he was in the hospital after Dieppe. General Donovan almost said as much to the SOE liaison at Duxford."

"That may be true. If it is, he is still a traitor. I have other concerns, which I will keep to myself for now. Just keep your eyes open, OK?"

"I always do. General, so nice to see you. General Gubbins, this is Lieutenant Colonel Stillwater from Duxford."

"Nice to meet you, Stillwater. I see that you are a history buff," the general said to him with a wink while pointing at Gibbons's *Decline and Fall of the Roman Empire, Volume III*, that he was holding.

"Yes, in fact I am, and I am afraid you caught me trying to impress Miss Andrich with my knowledge," Stillwater said, winking back.

"Well, I suppose we should all head over to the parlor. A young woman of your beauty dressed for dinner is a rare treat for most of these chaps. Make sure to keep your eyes open, Miss Andrich," the general said with a wink to her.

"He heard you," Trudy whispered urgently in Allen's ear.

"I certainly hope so. If the library isn't bugged, these guys are much dumber than I thought."

"Oh, so...I get it. Let's grab a drink," Trudy said as she entered the parlor.

The room went silent for a moment as Trudy entered behind the general. Colonel Scott spoke up first as he walked straight to Trudy, stepping in front of Rod.

"Miss Andrich, what can I get you to drink?"

"Vodka neat, in a tall glass," Trudy responded.

The colonel's eyes seemed to grow bigger for a moment, and Rod, standing behind him, had a similar reaction.

"I believe that we do have some very good Russian vodka, or would you prefer Finnish?" the colonel offered after regaining his composure.

"I would prefer Khortytsa, but the Russian vodka will be fine," Trudy replied.

"Did you say Khortytsa? I don't believe that I have heard of that. Is it a brand or type?" the colonel asked.

"It's an old Ukrainian brand," Trudy said politely.

"Oh, well, then, would Nemiroff be all right? It is another Ukrainian brand."

"That will be wonderful. Thank you, Colonel," Trudy said as she turned to Allen while the colonel headed to the bar.

"They certainly did their homework," Trudy whispered to Allen.

"Yes, they almost got it right, didn't they?" Allen whispered back.

"A lack of attention to detail on our part," Colonel Scott said as he returned with Trudy's vodka.

"I am flattered that you tried so hard to make me comfortable. Thank you," Trudy said.

"That kind of lack of attention to detail can get people killed in other settings. It is a good lesson for us all. *Za milyh dam*," Colonel Scott toasted as he raised his gin and tonic.

"*Vashe zdorovie*," Trudy said as she raised her vodka and took a quick gulp.

Allen raised a glass of champagne that he grabbed from a footman's serving tray. "Cheers to you both. To victory in combat."

"Here, here, to victory in combat!" several others in the group replied as they hoisted their drinks.

As a variety of toasts rang out, each seemed to stray closer and closer to subjects uncommonly discussed in mixed company. The bell again rang out, perhaps a bit more emphatically this time, by the now blushing butler, who was unaccustomed to feminine presence at a military "dining in."

Rod looked at his watch and verified that it had been rung a minute or two early and smiled about the situation. Trudy noticed his amusement after seeing Rod check his watch, and she smiled back at Rod as he glanced in her direction and waved for her to proceed into the dining room.

Trudy stepped forward and noticed that Colonel Scott had once again beat her to the table and was holding her chair.

"You are a true gentleman," Trudy complimented the colonel as she was once again seated next to the general at the head of the table.

"Please, everyone, sit down," the general instructed in a loud, commanding voice as he remained standing. There was a hurried seating of all guests, most with drinks still in hand from the parlor, with their toasts suddenly cut short.

"Thank you all for this marvelous example of Allied cooperation. There were many marvelous toasts a few moments ago, but I want to refocus us all on the job at hand with one last toast. To the success of Operation Stinger and the safe return of Major Roderick Jackson and Miss Trudy Andrich!" The general raised his glass, and the united group responded.

The butler then announced, "Dinner is served," and at least six footmen hurried plates to the table in volleys. Wine flowed, food was superb, and the camaraderie of arms was celebrated by all in a very traditional "dining in."

Trudy paced her drinks, knowing that there would be more alcohol served after dinner. She knew that she was the focus of attention in a loose-knit pack made up of prominent members of the warrior culture.

As the after-dinner port was passed around, increasingly solemn conversation occurred. Colonel Scott took the opportunity and whispered in Trudy's ear: "I need to speak with you privately for a few minutes. Can we make it look like I'm being a fool for a moment?" the colonel requested.

Trudy was initially suspicious, but there was a note of sincerity and sobriety in the colonel's voice that prompted her to trust him.

"Of course I would like to see a two-hundred-year-old wine collection," Trudy said loudly enough for Rod, the general, and Lieutenant Colonel Stillwater to hear. They all looked shocked except for the general.

Colonel Scott was also surprised for a moment by Trudy's fast and off-the-cuff response, but he recovered quickly and rose to help Trudy with her seat.

Colonel Scott led the way out of the dining room to the kitchen and the stairs that led to the wine cellar as several eyebrows were raised, and one of the captains smirked.

The colonel led the way down the dimly lit stairs into the wine cellar. It smelled musty but was well lit to reveal the dirt-floored cellar with row after row of valuable bottles.

"How did you know we had a wine cellar? That was a bit of a gamble." The colonel laughed as they stood facing each other at the bottom of the stairs.

"Well, of course you had a wine cellar! This is an English estate. Now please explain why this deception was needed, or I will scream and scream loudly."

"I assure you that there is no reason to scream. First of all, I am not the slightest bit interested in your type...of, uh, of woman."

"Well, that makes me feel so much better," Trudy said sarcastically, toying with him a bit but letting him off easy since he seemed to be inferring an alternate sexual preference.

"Really, Miss Andrich, this is quite important. I know that you were undoubtedly briefed that SOE was against this mission. We also know that you have some doubts about Major Jackson's loyalty, due to his previous affiliations."

"Go on," Trudy acknowledged and nodded.

"First, I want to assure you that Major Jackson has been informed in the strongest possible terms that SOE is one hundred percent behind this Allied plan that you were briefed on today."

"That is good to know, and I will pass that along," Trudy responded in a very businesslike tone.

"Lastly, I need to share, on a very personal level, that I have concerns about Major Jackson's commitment to this mission, probably for some of the same reasons that you may have developed doubts."

"Battle fatigue?" Trudy inquired.

"That has crossed my mind, too, but all I'll say now is that the reasons for some of his recent poor decisions seem a bit more complex."

"I agree, and I appreciate your candor. Now, you had better select a really good wine to explain our absence," Trudy said a little sternly.

"I already have one in mind, and I assure you that the chef would not have spared a Rothschild for this group on his own," the colonel said smiling as he pulled a bottle of Chateau Rothschild off the wine shelf and headed up the stairs.

Trudy laughed out loud and followed the colonel back into the dining room where he displayed the bottle to the general before handing it to one of the footmen to open.

"My god, but you have good taste!" the general said with a proud smile.

The Chateau Rothschild was split between Trudy, Colonel Scott, the general, and Major Jackson as the rest of those gathered around the table finished off several bottles of port.

When the bottle of Rothschild was finished, the general quietly excused himself and went off to his study. Those at the table were now free to disperse into the parlor, the library, or even outside into the cold night air.

Most went to the parlor. Trudy, Rod, Colonel Scott, and Lieutenant Colonel Stillwater went to the library to bid one another good night.

"Trudy, Rod, I will probably be asleep when you head back to Duxford early tomorrow morning, so Godspeed to both of you. You are a fantastic team," the colonel said as he shook hands and headed off to bed.

Trudy was next and bid goodnight to Rod and Lieutenant Colonel Stillwater as the two officers sat down in very comfortable chairs and Rod fidgeted with the latch on a cigar box.

CHAPTER 17
Cambridge, England, 18 1400 February 1944

The next afternoon, Trudy was dropped off at her flat in Cambridge by an SOE driver. Rod would be dropped off next. Trudy was a little bit embarrassed that she had fallen asleep during the ride and woke up with her head on Rod's shoulder. Rod smiled but almost pretended that it wasn't even noticed.

"All right, Trudy, it looks like we are on. I will see you at Duxford Saturday afternoon," Rod said as he straightened out the sleeve of his uniform jacket to pull out the wrinkles from where Trudy had been resting her head.

"I'll see you then." Trudy smiled back at Rod and then got out and thanked the driver for getting her bags out of the boot.

Trudy made her way up the stairs and unlocked the door of her flat. There was an envelope that someone had slipped under the door, so she picked it up, hurried inside, and, after locking the door behind her, opened the envelope. Inside was a handwritten note.

Trudy, sorry that I missed you again. I hoped that we can have a fun evening out before you leave. I know it will be soon.

Love, Rich

Trudy pulled out her notebook and dialed Ryan's number before she did anything else. Ryan picked up on the third ring at his Duxford office.

"Captain Ryan speaking," he answered formally.

"Rich, thank you so much for leaving me a note. I have been out of town."

"I heard through the grapevine that you were visiting with our allies. How about a fun night out?"

"As long as it is not a stuffy formal English dinner. I had a wonderful time, but I am ready to let my hair down a bit."

"I know just the place. We'll go to the Rex Ballroom. Can I pick you up at seven?"

"That will be perfect," Trudy replied.

"All right, then, see you tonight."

"At seven," Trudy repeated before she hung up.

Trudy had picked up some new clothing during her walks on nonflying days and had found a barely used blue patterned swing dress and matching shoes. They would be perfect for a night of dancing in GI-filled bars, as long as she had a date like Rich.

Trudy spent the afternoon getting her things sorted to pack for Duxford and bought a few things she found she needed since she would be spending the night there before takeoff on Sunday morning.

By seven Trudy was organized and ready for her date. With the details behind her, she was ready for a night on the town. Trudy fussed with her makeup in the bathroom for the third time when she heard the knock on the door. She checked for lipstick on her teeth and hurried to the door.

"Captain, you look stunning," Trudy commented to Rich, who was wearing his Pink and Greens with rows of ribbons on his uniform that seemed out of place for his age and rank.

"You look great, too, Trudy! I am so glad that you have time for a night out," Rich said with a broad smile.

"Would you like to come in for a drink before we head out?"

"Actually, I have a cab waiting for us at the curb. Should I send him on his way?"

"No, of course not. I'm famished, so let's go," Trudy said as she grabbed Rich's hand and pulled the door closed behind her.

It was a quick taxi ride to the Rex Ballroom, and Rich had reserved a table for two. The waiter recommended the roast beef or the cod. Trudy had the cod, and Rich went for the roast beef, both served with Brussels sprouts and potatoes.

"This food is amazing. It is a taste of home for me," Trudy said as she pointed at the cod.

"The food is great, but I have never gotten used to the northern cold-water fish. Back home, my favorite fish was grouper or red snapper."

"Where did you grow up, Rich?"

"Miami Springs, Florida, right on the edge of the Everglades. Our city was founded by someone you might even be familiar with: Glenn Curtiss?"

"I have heard of him; he is a real aviation pioneer. Did you ever meet him?"

"No, I never got the opportunity, but he has a mansion over by the golf course that people call the Alamo because of the unusual construction."

"Sounds like he was building to defend against the hurricanes instead of Santa Ana's Mexican army."

"You might be right; we do get some doozies. Afterward the streets are flooded for days, and people use boats to get around."

"How long does it take to get the water out of your basements?" Trudy asked with a concerned look.

"Basements? Nobody has basements. They would be flooded all the time. We are only about six feet above sea level. We build our houses up a few feet, so when it inevitably floods, it usually won't get in the house."

"Well, that doesn't sound too bad then, but I have heard the storms bring snakes?"

"Snakes, alligators, you name it. That's all just part of being a Florida Cracker."

"I hope that I can visit there someday. I have also heard that Miami Beach is beautiful."

"I would love to show it to you, Trudy."

The conversation tapered off as the two finished their meals. After the main course was done and plates were taken away, Rich pulled a present wrapped in newspaper out of his jacket pocket.

"Trudy, I want you to have this for your mission. There is an FP-45 single-shot .45-caliber pistol, which will be easy to conceal in your flight suit. There is also a flat double-edged dagger that you can tape to your arm or leg. These have saved my ass a time or two, and I want you to have them. Just don't open them here, OK?"

"Rich, thank you so much. I will be OK, though. Don't worry, all right?"

"I have done this a time or two before, and it is never what we expect, so always have a backup plan. Enough of this, though. Put that in your purse, and let's finish our food and dance the night away."

"Rich, you are a bit of a history buff. Do you know much about the Spanish Civil War?" Trudy asked innocently.

"As a matter of fact, I do. I'll bet you are interested in the airplanes."

"As a matter of fact, I am. I know that the Germans provided aircraft to the Nationalists. Where did the Republican side get their aircraft, from the United States?"

"Nope, not us. The Republicans got their planes from the Russians. Polikarpov fighters and Tupolev bombers, to name a few," Rich said proudly.

"So, it really was a testing ground for the war that was to come, for Germany and Russia?"

"You bet it was. It was a testing ground for our types, too. The Russians sent the NKVD, and the Germans sent Abwehr and Gestapo."

"And Americans who had missed the Great War flocked to Spain to get a taste of war. Amazing, isn't it?" Rich glanced at a beautiful English woman dancing with a GI.

"Gorgeous young woman with that lieutenant," Trudy commented to tease Rich a little bit.

"She really knows how to dance, doesn't she?" Rich replied sheepishly.

"I'm afraid that I'm not at that skill level," Trudy said with a laugh.

"That's good because I'm not either."

The band was playing some Glenn Miller tunes, and the dance floor was getting packed as they finished their meals along with their third beers. Trudy noticed some overly tense American military police come in through the front door. The sergeant in charge took a quick look at a photo in his palm and then surveyed the room as Trudy watched curiously. The sergeant made eye contact with Trudy, and Trudy got a very funny feeling that the MPs were there for her.

The three MPs headed straight to Trudy, and the sergeant stepped next to her table.

"Miss Andrich?"

"Yes, that is me," Trudy replied.

"You need to come with me now," the sergeant commanded.

"Now, wait a minute. What is this about, Sergeant?" Rich said standing up.

"Sir, you can shut the fuck up. If you say another word, my men here are gonna knock you out. Got it?"

"Sergeant, nobody is going anywhere until you explain what is going on," Rich said as he grabbed the nightstick out of the air as it swung toward his head and used it to choke and disable the MP who had been behind him. In the time that it took to do that, the sergeant had pulled out his Colt .45 and was pointing it at Rich's head.

"I ain't never shot an officer before, but it looks like tonight is the night," the sergeant uttered under his breath as more MPs flooded into the ballroom. "Now, Miss Andrich, you are going back to your apartment to collect your things, and we are going to Duxford. Is that clear? Because I will shoot you, too, if I have to."

Rich nodded to Trudy and the MPs, and Trudy gave Rich an evil look as she picked up her purse, which contained a gun that would definitely get her thrown in jail if it was discovered.

"This had better not be a setup," Trudy said sourly as she started to follow the MP sergeant.

"I didn't do this," Rich said as the MP who he had put to sleep climbed back to his feet and knocked Rich out with his baton.

As she walked outside with the MPs, Trudy noted that the bumpers of three MP jeeps did indicate that they were from Duxford, and she felt better but wondered what Rod had done to precipitate this and possibly scrub the mission. The MP helped her into the middle jeep, and, to her surprise, they did not handcuff her.

"OK, miss, weezz takin' you to your apartment furst, so youze can get your stuff," the sergeant instructed as the jeeps pulled away and headed toward Trudy's flat.

At her apartment, Trudy got out and was followed up to the front door by the sergeant.

"Don't try and use the phone or nothing like that, OK? I gotta get you to Duxford without any damage, according to my orders."

Trudy finished packing and handed the bag to the sergeant for him to carry.

"You can carry this, then," Trudy said as she maintained control of her purse, which contained the knife and single-shot pistol.

The sergeant complied without argument and loaded Trudy's bag into the back of the middle jeep after she got into the back seat. The sergeant jumped into the passenger seat and waved before the three jeeps took off at breakneck speed and headed out of Cambridge toward Duxford.

CHAPTER 18

Duxford, England, 18 2230 February 1944

At the front gate of Duxford, the jeeps didn't even slow down, and Trudy was glad that she had not jumped out of the speeding jeep as she had been considering. On base, they headed straight for base operations, and the MPs quickly escorted Trudy to Colonel Campbell's office.

Rod was sitting in a chair in front of Colonel Campbell's desk, asleep and looking like he had slept in his clothes for days.

"Here she is, sir," the MP sergeant announced proudly.

"Thank you, Sergeant," Colonel Campbell replied as he waved for the MP to leave.

"Trudy, I am really sorry to disturb your last free night before the mission, but we have a slight emergency. Please slap Rod, and wake him up."

Trudy reluctantly chose to shake Rod instead, and he woke slowly.

"Cynthia?" Rod uttered before he was fully awake.

"We don't even want to know who Cynthia is, Major Jackson. Now, wake up. This is important," Colonel Campbell said sternly.

"Yes, sir. I'm awake," Rod said wearily.

Trudy stood next to Rod looking a bit disgusted but alternately trying to keep a smile from breaking through.

"There has been an urgent change in our schedule. There is a strong front moving in from the northwest, and we expect that Duxford will be completely socked in by six on Sunday morning. We need you to get your planes in the air at a reasonable time tomorrow morning and fly them to

Leiston, where you will join the 357th Fighter Group. It actually simplifies things for you to sit in their briefing on mission day and take off with them. Our original plan had you flying there on the morning of the mission and linking up with them in the air before they joined up with the bombers that they will be escorting. This is just simpler, and the front is not expected to reach Leiston until Sunday evening. Unfortunately, Upwood is already socked in with heavy fog, and we don't expect the 156th Pathfinder Force (PFF) to be able to lead the mission."

"So, how badly do you think it will put us off course and away from the target?" Rod asked, as he slowly woke up.

"It all depends. The B-17s in the 447th have been on quite a few missions now, and their navigators have a good track record. It honestly probably won't make any difference. We wanted the extra level of certainty, due to the importance of this mission, but, as the English are fond of saying, we will carry on."

"Briefing at 1000, sir?" Trudy suggested.

"That sounds reasonable, but how about 0800 instead? Now, you two get some sleep. If that front comes in faster than expected and sits on us, we will need to taxi your Mustangs all the way to Leiston. I will have an orderly come wake you up at 0630 so you have time for breakfast before the briefing. Dismissed."

Trudy and Rod grabbed their bags and followed a waiting orderly to temporary quarters. This would be a short night.

Trudy felt like her head had just hit the pillow when insistent knocking on the door jarred her from a troubling dream that she couldn't quite remember.

"OK, I'm awake," she yelled as she woke.

"Breakfast in the canteen in ten minutes, miss," the orderly yelled through the door.

CHAPTER 19
Leiston, England, 19 0900 February 1944

Rod led the flight from Duxford to Leiston, and after contacting the tower, they requested a touch and go. The tower granted their request, and after a quick touch of the landing gear on the runway, Rod and Trudy went to full power. The upgraded engine of the P-51D sounded even stronger than the P-51Bs used by the local pilots, and many of the residents of the base stopped to looked to see what kind of aircraft was buzzing the base. Trudy and Rod entered the pattern after the touch and go and made conventional landings before a short taxi to the ramp in front of the tower that served as a temporary parking area for visiting aircraft.

Trudy unstrapped and crawled out of the cockpit onto the wing and was just about to jump down.

"Holy moly, look at the tail wheel on that," a young corporal yelled out to his buddy.

"Looks like she can handle a stick all right," a private replied.

"At ease there, soldier," a young captain in flight gear said as he walked past the young corporal and private. A couple of first lieutenants, also in flight gear, were following the captain.

The captain noticed the major's insignia on Rod as he got closer, and the young officers saluted him as they made a beeline for Trudy.

"Is this the new Mustang, miss? I didn't know it was going to be a two-seater," the captain said with a puzzled look on his face.

"It's an experimental version. We added the extra seat for an engineer observer," Trudy lied.

"It's only got two guns!" one of the lieutenants exclaimed.

"Don't worry; that's just a feature of this experimental version. The standard P-51D that you will be getting soon will have six Brownings, and they have mounted them upright in a redesigned wing so that you won't have the jamming problem with the machine guns that a lot of pilots have been complaining about. The D model also has the new K-14 gyroscopic gunsight that calculates how much to lead the enemy when you are in a turn."

"That will be a big improvement. The B version that we have now only has four Brownings, and at least one jams on almost every mission," the lieutenant replied.

"That's because you always fly straight and level. That new gunsight will be wasted on you, too. If you turned and banked more, the Brownings would be upright and wouldn't jam on you so often," one of the other lieutenants cracked.

"What's your name, ma'am?" the captain asked.

"Trudy Andrich."

"Wow, beautiful and rich," one of the lieutenants quipped.

"I think I have heard that one before, Lieutenant. What is your name?" Trudy replied while still maintaining her smile.

"Chuck, ma'am."

Rod stepped up next to Trudy.

"Take a good look, men; it won't be here for long. We'll be flying the mission with you boys tomorrow, and then we are off to another place," Rod announced.

"Did he mean the dame or the airplane, I wonder?" one of the lieutenants joked.

"That would be both, wise guy," Rod barked out. "Now we're going inside to check in, but we'll probably both hang out at the club with you guys tonight and will be happy to answer any questions about the planes."

"That will be swell, sir. We are supposed to get D models by the end of August. The extra visibility with that bubble canopy is gonna make a big difference for us, too. We have a blind spot straight behind us now as you probably know, sir."

"We'll see you men later," Rod said as he returned salutes from the young officers and headed to base operations. Trudy caught up and walked beside him on his left as she had noticed was advisable since Rod would likely be returning more salutes with his right arm.

After arrangements were made for topping off the tanks on the Mustangs and basic maintenance checks, Rod and Trudy went back to their planes to collect the rest of their gear. There were at least twenty pilots poring over the planes by the time they made their way back to them, and they stayed around to answer questions and talk about tactics with the pilots for more than an hour before they took their gear to the visiting officers' quarters and then went to the Officers' Club for lunch.

After lunch, Rod and Trudy spent the afternoon visiting the 357th Fighter Group's commander Colonel Spicer and Major Throop, commander of the 363rd fighter squadron, which they would be flying with in the morning.

Trudy and Rod both agreed to make it an early night since they had no expectation of getting a good night's sleep after they landed in Lithuania.

In spite of their best intentions, Rod and Trudy stayed at the club until after eleven. They felt a special obligation to the pilots who would be protecting them in the morning. The atmosphere of the traditional English pub had been adapted for the Officers' Club. Relics from past missions, memorials to those lost, and an endless flow of beer in the packed bar made it a place of comfort, too, for warriors living far from home.

As the evening wound down and they said goodnight, the squadron commander provided some sage advice: "Just take some pure oxygen after you get strapped in, and it will do wonders for clearing your head up. Best hangover cure I ever found," he said as he shook hands with Trudy and Rod.

"Goodnight, everyone," Trudy waved as she departed. Many of the pilots raised their glasses to toast her in return.

CHAPTER 20

Leiston, England, 20 0500 February 1944

Trudy and Rod were awakened by an orderly at 0400. By 0430 they were dressed and at the chow hall for coffee, fried hash, and eggs. Neither Rod nor Trudy was very hungry, but both also understood the need for a healthy meal before a long day of flying. By 0500 Trudy and Rod were seated in the front row of the briefing room on slightly uncomfortable folding chairs.

Colonel Spicer, the 357th Fighter Group commander, jumped up on the narrow three-foot-high stage with a long wooden pointer in hand. As the colonel stepped onto the stage, a major in the back yelled, "At ease," to quiet the room.

"OK, men and Miss Andrich, today is the start of Operation Argument or, as most of the brass are calling it, 'Big Week.' This will be a major push against targets deep inside Germany by the Mighty Eighth. The mission today is named Tutow. Today, 304 B-17s from the 94th Bomber Group, 95th Bomber Group, 96th Bomber Group, 100th Bomber Group, 385th Bomber Group, 388th Bomber Group, 390th Bomber Group, our friends at the 447th Bomber Group, and the 452nd Bomber Group will be on the mission. It's the heart of the German aircraft industry, just outside of or, more accurately, about sixty miles east of Rostock and about twenty miles from the Baltic coast of Germany. It's also where they make the FW-190s, so let's hope the B-17s give 'em hell today," the colonel said, pointing at the town of Rostock on the map before continuing. "We will be escorting the 447th Bomber Group, flying out of Rattlesden just east of us here. Their B-17s were supposed to have some Lancasters from the 156th Pathfinders, but they are socked at their base at Upwood and won't be able to join the party today. Duxford is socked in, too, Major, so it was a smart move to fly down here yesterday," he said while looking at Rod.

"The 447th will be taking off just before 0730, and it will take them at least twenty minutes to get all their planes in the air. We will take off at 0730, and by the time we form up in the air and head up to Rattlesden, they will be on their way. Our sequence of the groups' three squadrons will be a little different today, due to our guests. The 364th will take off first and lead the group, followed by the 362nd, and the 363rd will take off last. Once in the air, the 362nd will trail with the 363rd in the middle. I will fly with the 363rd today with our guests. Our official linkup will be at this point right on the coast. The experimental Mustangs will be with us until we get to Rostock, and then they will be taking care of some other business, so don't try to follow them. At that point, just stick with the bombers, and make sure that they get back in one piece. On the way in, we will be flying well north of Helgoland to avoid the flak towers, which means that we will be crossing the Danish peninsula up north here near Flensburg. When we get back over water, the bombers will descend to their bombing altitude of twelve thousand feet. The bombers will be dropping a mix of incendiary and general-purpose bombs. Frequencies, call signs, and headings will be on the mission data card handed out on the way out, so don't forget to pick yours up, Lieutenant Korman. Any questions? All right, S-2, what are we facing today?"

The S-2 provided a quick threat briefing, which was followed by a detailed weather briefing.

The group commander then jumped back on the stage. "Miss Andrich, when the pilots head to the ready room to get into their flying gear, you can head to my office, and my orderly has been instructed to guard the door," Colonel Spicer said before he jumped down off the stage.

"Hack watches," he said as he looked at his watch. Everyone else in the room aligned the minute and second hands to exactly 0530 and waited for their commander's countdown as he focused on his wristwatch.

"Ten, nine, eight, seven, six, five, four, three, two, one, hack! That is all. Dismissed!"

At the end of the formal briefings, the pilots flooded out the door, each picking up a mission data card from a sergeant standing at the door to the briefing room.

There was a mad rush to the ready room and the pilots' lockers. As the male pilots got dressed in the crowded ready room, Trudy used the privacy of the colonel's office to conceal the backup single-shot .45 pistol and extra ammo that Rich had provided. She also taped the flat dagger to her calf, just above her boot. With her flight suit, G-suit, and shoulder holster on, Trudy pulled on her leather jacket and Mae West life preserver and then headed to the arms room to pick up her issue pistol. At the arms room, the armorer tried to give her a .38 revolver.

"I'm not taking that gun anywhere near Germany," Trudy declared.

"Well, you need to carry a gun; it's regulations," the armorer replied in a tired voice.

"Of course I am going to carry a gun. I want a .45 Colt, not some girly little revolver," Trudy declared.

"Miss, you can't shoot one of those; that's a man's gun," the armorer declared indignantly.

"I shot thirty out of thirty when I qualified expert with a .45 M-1911, so don't argue with me," Trudy said impatiently.

"Give her the .45, Sergeant; she won't need to shoot it anyhow," a captain who had joined the line behind her said impatiently.

The armorer handed the .45 M-1911 Colt to Trudy along with three magazines, each containing seven rounds of .45-caliber ammo.

"Did you really shoot thirty out of thirty?" the captain asked as they left the line.

"Of course I did," Trudy responded.

"How did you handle the recoil? Excuse me for saying this, but even though you are tall, you don't have a lot of meat on your bones."

"It's simple, Captain. Just bend your elbows a little bit, and let your arms move back slightly with the recoil. If you lock your elbows like the army drill sergeants teach you, the recoil will raise your arms and make you bend at the shoulders instead of taking up the shock with your arms."

"Thanks, I'll try that next time I qualify," the captain said, as he waved and ran off to his airplane.

By seven, pilots were climbing into their airplanes, and by seven fifteen they began starting their engines. Trudy and Rod were slated to take off last to conserve fuel. At seven thirty the first Mustang took off, and all forty-eight planes were in the air within fifteen minutes. The sound of the entire group of Mustangs was deafening.

Trudy and Rod followed the other Mustangs and took up positions in the middle of the formation, as they had been instructed. Trudy could see the stalled weather front that had chased them out of Duxford.

The thirty-six B-17s from the 447th Bomber Group were already formed up to the east and were departing the pattern above Rattlesden Field. The other bomber groups were soon seen in the sky. The bombers leveled off at twenty-two thousand feet, and the Mustangs soon caught up with them and broke into escort formations to protect the bombers from above. The Mustangs were in three tight "V" formations as they headed out over the North Sea at twenty-five thousand feet. No enemy contact was expected until they approached the Danish coast.

As the bombers approached the Danish coast, the black puffs of flak from German antiaircraft guns appeared below them. The bombers remained on course and stayed in tight formation in spite of the flak. The Mustangs changed course several times while keeping the bombers in sight to confuse enemy radar.

Black smoke erupted from the engine of a B-17 in the 385th Bomber Group. The smoke trail followed the B-17 as it descended and turned in the direction of England, a victim of a random piece of shrapnel.

As they crossed the Danish coastline along the Baltic, the bombers began their descent to the prescribed twelve-thousand-foot bombing altitude. Another thirty minutes went by, and there was still no sign of enemy fighters. The thick clouds below explained the absence of the Luftwaffe. Those same clouds that kept the Luftwaffe grounded also obscured the target, and the lead bombardier understood that his bomb drop would be based on timing and estimated position. Lieutenant Chestnut checked his watch and took another quick glance in the bomb sight with a faint hope of seeing the target or even a small piece of land.

"Bombs away," the lieutenant yelled into the radio, and 304 bombers dropped their loads based on the Kentucky windage of a first lieutenant and his wristwatch.

Trudy and Rod drove away from the formation and began their low-level approach to Lithuania across a cloud-covered Baltic Sea. At less than one thousand feet, they leveled off and stayed within fifty yards of each other so that they would not become separated in the thick layer of haze.

At one thousand feet, it was a bumpy ride with a strong wind coming from the north. Konigsberg would be in sight within an hour. Trudy and Rod knew that they would need to be north of Konigsberg, and they hoped to see it emerge on their right side.

After a little bit over an hour of flying low over the water, Trudy was getting tired from flying the plane in the bumpy air. She was also getting a little bit worried that they had not seen land yet when she saw a forested peninsula with a line of low barrier islands stringing northward. Konigsberg would be at the base of that peninsula. As she had feared, the wind from the north had pushed them almost fifty miles south of their intended flight path. The navigation error offered them a slight advantage, though. As Trudy turned north to avoid Konigsberg and started a climb to six thousand feet, she realized that if she was picked up on radar at this point, she would appear to be leaving the northern coast of Poland from a city like Gdansk. On this flight path, the Germans were unlikely to send up interceptors.

Trudy wanted to share her insight about their newfound luck, but they needed to maintain radio silence, or all bets were off. Rod had not seen land yet by the time Trudy started her turn north since he was focused on his right, feeling very certain about his navigation skills. He did see Trudy turn, though, as she climbed above him, and he reacted immediately to set a parallel course, now seeing the tree-covered hills on the peninsula.

In another fifteen minutes, both Trudy and Rod could see past the barrier islands to the Lithuanian mainland. Trudy noticed a change in the color of the water that marked where the Neman River poured into the Baltic Sea. She knew that north of the Neman was Lithuania with the mouth of the river marking the border with Poland. Since the river drifted slightly southward, Trudy corrected her course once more to cross the Baltic coast over Poland, keeping the Neman River north of her until the point where it turned and meandered almost due east.

Back over land, Rod led Trudy back down to two thousand feet, and they were now almost directly over the river. With both Trudy and Rod concentrating on finding their way, they missed the two aircraft diving at them from above. Rod made a sharp turn to the right, which Trudy mirrored. Neither of them understood why the fighter that had jumped them did not fire until they saw the red stars painted on the wings and fuselage of the two Yakovlev YAK-3s.

Trudy was immediately frightened, and she knew that their mistake could have proven deadly and might still. Rod got back on course following the river, and both Trudy and Rod watched as the YAK-3s turned, and this time, instead of a gun run, they set a parallel course as if they were joining a formation on the left side of the Mustangs. The YAK-3 pilot on the right pulled close to Trudy, and Trudy waved her wings. The female YAK pilot smiled and gave thumbs-up in admiration for the new American airplane and out of surprise at seeing an American woman pilot. Trudy saw her make a call on the radio, and the two YAKs accelerated and climbed toward Russia.

"That was a close call," Trudy muttered to herself.

Another twenty minutes went by, and Rod was the first to see the point in the river where it made a sharp turn south. And he descended to thousand feet before he made his turn south at that point directly over the small village listed on the map as Vilkija. Trudy noticed the twin steeples of the Roman Catholic Church in the center of Vilkija as she made her turn south, following Rod.

As they continued south, Trudy could see the smoke from many chimneys on the horizon due east of her, and she suspected that she was seeing Kaunas, where they would meet the professor. As the river made a sharp turn back east, Trudy was certain that the smoke was from Kaunas, and she started looking for the smoke that would mark their landing site to the south of the river. Trudy saw what looked like smoke to the south now, but she could not determine the source. As she flew farther south, Trudy finally saw the patchwork landscape where peat farms had been cut out of a swampy-looking forest.

Rod had seen the smoke, too, and he descended to less than five hundred feet to make a low pass parallel to the string of six or seven peat mounds that were emitting white smoke. Rod saw a man on a tractor wave and then raise both arms and move his hands up and down with his hands outstretched to indicate the path of the runway. Rod noted that the winds were next to nonexistent at the moment since the smoke from the peat mounds was going almost straight up.

Rod made one more low pass and then made a turn south of the landing strip that put him on an approach to the landing strip. Trudy circled to provide security. She watched as Rod made his approach and then touched down, making small clouds of dust where his main landing gear touched.

"Well, at least it's dry," Trudy said to herself as she continued to orbit the landing strip and watch for signs of trouble.

Rod taxied his Mustang toward the series of long barns at the north end of the strip, and Trudy watched the man on the tractor wave. And then as Rod emerged from his aircraft, the two men shook hands. Trudy glanced away to check her altitude and airspeed. When she looked back to where Rod was standing, he had climbed up onto the tractor and was doing a one-handed wave that indicated it was safe for her to land. Trudy continued her orbit to the north of the landing strip and then flew south on a parallel course to the runway heading south. Well south of the landing strip, Trudy made a ninety-degree turn to the left for a short base leg of her landing pattern, followed almost immediately by another sharp ninety-degree turn that put her on final approach. Trudy noted that the smoke was still rising straight up from the peat fires to the right of the landing strip, so wind would not be a factor. Two minutes later, Trudy lowered her landing gear and touched down very close to the end of the strip, worried that she might hit Rod's Mustang if she used too much of the length of the strip.

Trudy stopped the Mustang next to Rod's plane, set the brakes, and shut down the engine. She unstrapped herself and felt for her Colt M-1911 under her jacket. She then pulled out the pistol, pulled back the slide, and chambered a round, leaving the hammer cocked on the single-action weapon but engaging the thumb safety before she returned the weapon to its holster under her jacket. Now ready for trouble, Trudy climbed out of the plane and jumped off the wing to greet Rod, who was now standing next to her airplane.

"Welcome to Lithuania, Trudy," Rod grinned for a moment after he spoke.

"Thanks," was Trudy's only reply as she surveyed the nearby tree line.

A moment later, the man emerged from in front of Trudy's Mustang, ducking under the propeller and making Trudy cringe at his unsafe action. The man was a little bit heavy, nearly six feet tall and with short, curly black hair. Trudy immediately recognized him as Jonas Necris from the photo that SOE had shown them.

"You must be Jonas," Trudy said in Russian.

"And you must be Trudy," Jonas replied. "My SOE contact said that you are a beautiful woman with blond hair who flies airplanes, so it must be you."

"What are we going to do about hiding these airplanes?" Rod said urgently.

"As soon as I finish putting out those fires with the tractor, I will come back and pull your airplanes between those two barns. We have canvas and rope that will act like a big tent between the barns. That will hide them from the air, but the Germans aren't doing much flying around here. Every time they fly, they die since the Russian front lines are so close."

"We ran into a couple of YAKs on the way here," Rod exclaimed. "That was quite a surprise."

"I think we surprised her as much as she surprised us," Trudy replied.

"Her? The pilot was a woman?" Rod exclaimed.

"Yes, that is not too surprising. They are using lots of women pilots since they are so short of men for the infantry," Jonas said. "So, you two can wait in the barn while I put out these fires. Dmitri is in there waiting for you. He was looking out to make sure this was not some kind of German trap."

"So, I guess I wasn't the only one who was worried," Trudy said to Rod in English.

"Let's stick with Russian from now on. It's too easy to slip up, OK?"

"OK, agreed," Trudy replied in Russian as they headed to the barn.

Trudy and Rod walked around the side of the barn where the tractor path led to open sliding doors. A skinny, gray-haired man with glasses and a wool cap stepped out in front of them holding a German ZF-41 sniper rifle. The man kept the weapon at port arms as he raised his right hand to wave briefly before grabbing the stock again instead of awkwardly holding the rifle with one hand.

"I am Dmitri. What is your name?" Dmitri said in very rough German as he stared at Trudy, seemingly ignoring Rod.

"I am Trudy, and this is Rod," Trudy said in Russian.

"Oh, you speak Russian! All the Englishmen who they send to work with us speak only German or English. What a pleasant surprise. I am not as worried about taking you to Kaunas now. Trudy, hold this for me please," Dimitri said as he handed Trudy the ZF-41 and walked around the corner of the barn. Trudy and Rod followed him between the two barns and watched curiously as Dmitri walked to the side of the barn and started untying a rope from a hitch on the side of the barn. Dmitri started to pull on the rope and looked disgustedly at Rod and Trudy, who were standing on a large sheet of canvas spread out between the two barns and partially covered with straw.

"Now, how do you expect me to hide your airplanes if you are standing on my canvas?" Dmitri said while waving his hands in the air.

Rod and Trudy jumped off the canvas, and Rod went over to help Dmitri pull on the rope to lift the canvas while Trudy stood guard with the ZF-41. There was a series of eight ropes and pulleys that had been put in place to lift two large sections of canvas. Rod and Dmitri raised the canvas with the ropes and pulled hard to make the canvas taut.

"This was a good idea, Dimitri," Trudy praised as Dmitri stood with hands on both hips while looking up and surveying the canvas.

"It was Jonas's idea, and it will be good if it does not rain hard or snow, which could happen this time of year. Rain or snow will break the ropes. But then you are not staying long, so I guess it will serve its purpose," Dmitri said as he stepped over to Trudy and held out his hand for his rifle. Trudy handed Dmitri the rifle.

"You mentioned that you would be taking us to Kaunas. We are going to need to change someplace," Trudy said.

"The Englishman said that you would be bringing some clothes to wear, but they never look right, so Jonas and I brought some used clothing from town."

"How did you know our sizes?" Rod said, looking puzzled.

"The Englishman said you were both tall. You are both military, so I knew you were not fat and I found clothes with very long sleeves and pants legs. Since I am a tailor, I will make them fit."

"That is going to take some time, though," Rod said impatiently.

"Rod, let me tell you one thing, OK? We are not going anywhere today. You two are going to rest at the house after I take your measurements, and tomorrow we will go to Kaunas. Farmers never go to town in the afternoon; they go to town in the morning, so that is when we will go. Besides, people who are tired do stupid things. A very little stupid thing will get us all killed in Kaunas."

"Are there lots of Gestapo in Kaunas?" Trudy asked.

"Who needs Gestapo? Kaunas has plenty of fascists, but yes, there are Gestapo there. Also the Gestapo are not what you might expect. They are not all running around like peacocks in those black uniforms. Most of them are dressed like the local people, and they are the ones who are watching the professor and others like him. They are also the most dangerous."

As Dmitri finished his sentence, Jonas came around the corner of the barn pulling Rod's Mustang by the tail wheel with a long braided rope. Jonas stopped and jumped down off the tractor and looked up at the canvas tents, inspecting them as he approached the others.

"I think we can fit them tail to tail. There is room on both sides for you to drive them out, but we will need to take down the canvas before you start your engines, or the wind that you make will tear them free and send them who knows where," Jonas said in a lecturing manner that made Trudy guess that he was either a father or a teacher.

"OK, Jonas, noted. We will help guide you in so we don't clip a wing or something dragging them in here," Rod advised.

"Yes, of course. I will pull this one in from that end and then pull the other one in from that side," Jonas replied.

"Jonas, you idiot. What are you talking about? How do I deserve such a dumb nephew? If you drag the second airplane in from the other side, you will not be able to get the tractor out past the wings," Dmitri said as he waved his fists furiously at the sky above at the feigned location of God.

"So, what do I need with the tractor while we are in town? It will hide it, too!" Jonas yelled back in Yiddish.

"Speak Russian, you dumb-ass!" Dimitri yelled back.

"Gentlemen, gentlemen, can't we please just get the planes in here? It won't matter which way the planes are facing; the tractor will still be stuck between the planes since we need to pull them by the tail. Facing in opposite directions is best, in case one of the planes won't start," Trudy said in a slow, calming voice.

"All right. I just hope that you don't need that tractor," Dimitri conceded.

It took another twenty minutes to get both Mustangs under cover, and it was getting to be dusk as Dimitri led Trudy, Rod, and Jonas down a path through the woods to a farmhouse. As the path opened into a clearing, a white masonry two-story house sat next to a small hilltop. There was smoke coming from the chimney, indicating that someone was home. Dimitri led the group through the front door.

"Angie, the guests are here," Dmitri announced as they entered the house.

The house was warm from the fire, and the smell of cooking beef and vegetables made Trudy hungry. She had been too busy to think about food until now. She also knew that in spite of the hospitality of their hosts, they were far behind enemy lines, and things could turn bad in an instant.

A short heavy woman with deep dimples on her cheeks entered the room. Her gray hair was pulled back in a bun, and she was wearing an apron with a butcher knife tucked into a scabbard that was sewn into the front pocket of the apron.

"Welcome to our home. They are tall; I think you guessed right about their clothing," Angie said as she looked Trudy and Rod up and down. "I know you must be hungry after flying here all the way from England, so please sit down after you wash up for dinner," Angie said as she pointed down the hallway to a washroom. "I filled the pitchers with water, and there is fresh soap, too," Angie said proudly.

All four lined up with Jonas going first to show Trudy and Rod how to properly use the pitchers and basins to wash and then how to dispose of the dirty water through the built-in indoor toilet.

As everyone got cleaned up, Angie had started to deliver heaping, steaming bowls of food to the table.

"I hope you are not kosher," Dmitri warned Rod. "I know she is not, but you might be."

Rod shook his head no, seemingly confused by the question.

"That's good, because we raise pigs and cook pork in the kitchen occasionally. It's a good way to keep the Nazis guessing. Today we have beef, which is special for you. If you two get us killed, we will have smiles on our faces when we meet God from the good food," Dimitri joked.

"After dinner, Dmitri will get your measurements, and he will work on your clothing during the night. We will get up when it is light, and I will take you into town in our wagon. It will be cramped, but you can maybe even sleep more on the way." Jonas looked to see that Angie was not about to pop out of the kitchen and then whispered to Trudy and Rod as he leaned forward. "I told Angie that you were husband and wife so that she would put you in the same bedroom. The bedrooms are very cold except for the one I sleep in over the kitchen."

"That was very thoughtful of you, Jonas," Rod said with a smile.

"Yes, *thoughtful* might be one description," Trudy said as she kicked Rod under the table.

Angie made one last trip to the table, placing freshly baked bread on the table before she sat down. With everyone in place, Angie crossed herself, which prompted a puzzled look on Trudy's face.

"What? You think we are that good at acting like we are not Jews? Angie is Roman Catholic; I'm the Jew in the family," Dmitri said in a kidding tone.

"Uncle, fill your mouth with food instead of talking. The food is wonderful, Aunt Angie," Jonas said as he soaked some bread in the beef and turnip stew before filling his own mouth.

"The food is wonderful, Angie," Trudy said as she ate a slice of pickled beets after a mouthful of the beef and turnip stew.

"Thank you so much. Enjoy. Tomorrow will be a hard day, and I will say the Rosary for you every hour. Jonas, what time do you expect to be back?"

"Definitely before dark. Then we will have two more guests until the next morning."

"The professor is kosher. I have spoken with him a couple of times. A stubborn man but very brilliant. He doesn't see the connection between his work and what the Nazis want it for. I told him it's a betrayal of his people, so he doesn't like me. He just says that it is science, and he thinks he is above all the politics. Really dumb idea for a brilliant guy to have."

"Dmitri, you are getting all worked up. If you make yourself sick, you won't be able to work on their clothes tonight," Angie cautioned.

"How long have you lived here?" Trudy asked Angie, to change the subject.

"This is the home I grew up in. I was the last one still in Lithuania when the second war started. The rest of the family went to America, so when Dmitri and I were married, the house became ours."

"We have had a good life here in spite of the war. The place isn't near any main roads, and the soldiers just go around our farm because of the swamp. Who would have thought that you could dig peat from a swamp and sell it to feed your family?"

"Great food, Angie," Rod said, having an empty mouth for the first time since they started eating. "You mentioned we would be taking a cart into town?"

"Yes, we built a peat and vegetable cart with a false bottom over the axle. The boards on the side of the cart hide the opening. We don't want you to use your papers at the Gestapo checkpoint since they have become very skilled at detecting forgeries for reasons we don't understand."

"They are not detecting forgeries, Jonas; they are expecting certain names. The English have a spy working for them," Dmitri lectured.

"Maybe so, uncle. This way will be best, in any case. We also have a backup plan to get home. There is a boat hidden near the college that will only fit four people, and the water is too cold to swim in now, so let's not have a need for the backup plan, OK?"

"Yes, let's hope not," Trudy said as she finished another mouthful of stew.

"If everyone has had enough, I will clean up while Dmitri does his tailoring," Angie said as she got up from the table.

"Thank you, Angie," Rod said as he stood up.

"Yes, thank you," Trudy said as she followed Dmitri over to the corner and stood on a measuring platform that seemed to be a fixture in the home.

Trudy looked at the window and saw her reflection in the glass. During dinner, darkness had fallen, and there was a new moon that had not yet risen for the evening, so it was pitch black, away from any city lights.

"That should do it," Dmitri pronounced. "Rod, you are next."

"I'll get ready for bed," Trudy said as she headed off to her room in a hurry. Her plan was to change before Rod was done with his measurements.

Jonas was right about the room being cold. The heat from the fire and the cooking stove rose up through a vent in the floor of Jonas's room and moved across the floor to the staircase. The floor and walls in the back bedroom assigned to Rod and Trudy were cold to the touch, and there was frost on the inside of the window already. Trudy changed underwear and decided to get back into her flight suit before she crawled under the two quilts on the twin bed just as Rod knocked briefly and came into the room without waiting for a response.

"I didn't catch you naked, did I?" Rod grinned.

"Hopefully you never will. I'm in my flight suit. It really is cold in here."

"When I get under the covers, too, we will both be warmer. If that doesn't work, some calisthenics under the covers might be called for."

"If you are thinking of push-ups, you can do them down by the fire to get warm," Trudy said with a laugh.

Rod turned his back as he stripped naked and crawled into bed before he turned down the kerosene lamp on the bedside table. Trudy smiled but covered her face so that Rod would not see her lack of disgust for his naked form.

Carly was right; he does have a nice ass, Trudy thought as she giggled out loud.

"Are you doing something that I should know about over there?" Rod said as he rolled over to face Trudy.

"No, I was just thinking about what a crazy day this has been," Trudy lied.

"And it is finally over. Are you warmer yet?"

"Yes, I believe that I am. Good night."

"Good night, Trudy."

CHAPTER 21

Ezerlis, Lithuania, 21 0430 February 1944

Trudy woke to a knock on the bedroom door.

"Breakfast is ready," Angie said from behind the door.

"Thank you. We'll be right down," Trudy said as she poked at Rod to wake him up.

Rod rolled over, and Trudy felt something poke her leg as Rod provided an innocent smile.

"Oh god, it is cold in this room," Trudy said as she jumped out of bed and pulled back all the covers. "It looks like you need to get dressed and use the facilities," Trudy joked as she pulled on her jacket. "I'll meet you at breakfast."

"The least you could do would be to replace the covers," Rod said in a perturbed voice.

"It's time to get up. I'll see you at breakfast," Trudy said as she exited the room, leaving Rod naked and uncovered on the bed.

"Well, fuck you, too," Rod uttered with a laugh.

Trudy closed the door. *Don't you wish*, she said to herself as she skipped down the stairs.

"Trudy, you get the first plate. I am adding potato to the turnip and beef and then frying it into cakes. We have eggs, too. Thankfully, we always have eggs. Dmitri will take some to market today and probably use some to bribe the guards at the checkpoint so they won't spend too much time with him."

Trudy held out a plate for Angie to place the golden-brown potato, turnip, and beef cake on her plate and headed to the table.

"Don't wait for me. Dimitri and Jonas have already eaten and are getting the cart loaded for the market. I'll have one of these ready for Rod when he comes down. Do you want me to do eggs, too?"

"Not for me. This is really filling. Delicious, too. I never would have thought of doing this."

"The Lord gives us what we need, but we can't be wasteful."

"This is really good. So, how did you and Dimitri meet?"

"Near the end of the Great War, Dimitri was in a barn fire and badly burned over much of his lower body. I was a nursing student. I was also studying to be a nun and worked at the hospital where they brought Dimitri. The mother superior assigned me to care for Dimitri and keep him alive, which seemed like an impossible challenge at the time. In the weeks and months ahead, he improved, and by the time he was well enough to be released, we had fallen in love. Instead of taking my vows to our Lord Christ, I took a vow to be with Dimitri until the end of our lives."

"What a wonderful story. It is obvious you have no regrets."

"No regrets. Dimitri was a blessing to me as I was for him."

"Good morning, Angie," Rod said as he bounded into the room off the stairs, seemingly full of energy.

"Good morning, Rod. I trust you slept well?" Angie inquired.

"Yes, very well, thank you."

"I made some breakfast for you; the others have already eaten, so fill your plate."

Rod was famished and started eating the potato-and-turnip cake on the way to the table with a fork he had grabbed in the kitchen.

Rod devoured the potato-and-turnip cake, and as he was finishing a glass of milk, Dimitri came in through the front door.

"Good morning. I have some clothes for you to change into before we go," he said, picking up a stack of folded cloths and handing them to Trudy. "Remember to change everything. If the Gestapo rips open your blouse to search you and you have English underclothes, you will be dead. I am sure that everything will fit," Dimitri said proudly.

"He has been doing tailoring for almost as long as he has been farming. Even the Germans in Kaunas sometimes pay for his services," Angie said proudly.

Trudy headed up the stairs. "Give me a few minutes, Rod," Trudy yelled over her shoulder as she headed up the stairs.

"Surely you have seen her dress before?" Angie said a little bit suspiciously.

"Certainly, but if Trudy sees me naked, she can't keep her hands off of me, and we don't have time for that now."

"Oh, I see," Angie said as she blushed and rushed into the kitchen.

Dimitri shook a finger at Rod. "You, sir, are quite a rascal."

Trudy came down the stairs in a classic A-line skirt and a white linen blouse and jacket under an open wool coat.

"Wow. You look amazing, but I don't think that you will pass for a farmer or even a farmer's daughter," Rod exclaimed.

"Remember, we are sneaking you into the city, but once you are there, you need to look like you belong at the university, where you will meet Professor Michalonis," Dmitri again lectured.

Rod nodded in agreement and went upstairs to change. In a few minutes, he came down the stairs in a fashionably rumpled wool suit and dress shoes that were just a tad too tight.

"You look like a Lithuanian history professor," Trudy said with a laugh as Rod seemed a little disappointed at the unfashionable loose cut of the heavy wool suit.

"Marvelous. I just now lined the hidden compartment in the cart with wool blankets and two pillows, so the clothing won't get snagged on the wood as long as you don't roll around too much."

"Where is Jonas?" Trudy asked.

"He is waiting outside. He says that if he comes in to warm up, it will make the ride even colder for him. I think he is crazy, but what do I know?"

"OK, let's go," Rod said as he headed out the door behind Dimitri.

"My prayers go with you all. Please take care of Dimitri," Angie said as she closed the door behind Trudy.

"We will," Trudy replied.

CHAPTER 22

Kaunas, Lithuania, 21 1000 February 1944

Trudy and Rod were both surprised by how rough the ride was in the cramped false bottom of the springless cart. Every pothole in the ancient dirt road bounced them into the top of the compartment. It was also cold. The thin wood sides and the gaps between the boards left for fresh air also brought in the cold from below. After several bounces that threatened to give them both broken noses or black eyes, Rod put his arms around Trudy and held her close. Trudy reciprocated, understanding their predicament, but soon she felt warm and safe in Rod's arms. They remained in an embrace for over an hour as the cart trundled along the rough country road.

Maybe he isn't that much of an asshole, Trudy thought, just as the cart slowed and then came to a stop.

"Halt, papers," a German Wehrmacht soldier demanded of Dimitri and Jonas as they stopped their horse cart. The checkpoint was at the south end of the bridge crossing the Neman into Kaunas.

Jonas and Dimitri sat on the bench seat of the wagon, holding their seventeen-hand mare in place with a quick tug on the reins. Jonas provided the papers for both Dimitri and himself.

"So, where are you going this morning?" the soldier questioned out of rote.

"We are going to the market. Here is a sample of the eggs we have," Jonas said as he handed a small box with three eggs in it to the soldier.

"Eggs? Maybe I should take them all before I let you pass," the soldier said to hopefully get a few more eggs.

"If you take them all, there will be none left for us to bribe the Gestapo with. I will tell them it is because you stole them," Dimitri said sternly to the soldier.

"Very well, you may pass," the soldier said as he waved them through the checkpoint.

Jonas steered the cart through the crowded city streets to the market in the center of town. Instead of going directly to their assigned seller's stall, Jonas guided the horse cart into a long barn behind the market. Once inside, Dimitri jumped down and began to feed and water the horse while Jonas pried off the side of the cart to allow Trudy and Rod to crawl out. Jonas motioned for them to stay low and for them to be quiet with a finger in front of his lips.

"When I motion from the alley that it is safe, stand up and walk normally to the left, down the alley. There is a cab there with one of my people driving. He will take you to the university. Do not take any other cabs. Many of the drivers work for the Gestapo. Now remember, if you are not here by sunset, we will meet you on the south riverbank in the wooded area just downstream from the university. We will wait for you in the woods so the guards on the bridge just west of there don't spot us. If you are not there by midnight, we will come back after dark the next day and wait until midnight once more; after that, you are on your own to find a way back to your airplanes. Do you understand?"

Trudy and Rod both nodded, and Jonas walked over to the barn entrance just as two farmers strolled past. Jonas waited for almost two minutes and then waved hurriedly for Trudy and Rod to come to him. When they got to Jonas, they stood up, and Jonas shook both their hands quickly as he directed them down the alley to the waiting taxi.

Trudy and Rod got into the back seat of the taxi from separate sides and pulled the doors closed. The elderly-looking man in the driver's seat did not turn his head but instead used the mirror. "Jonas said that you need to go to the university science building. I will drop you off in front and wait. Do not take another taxi," the old man said as he smoothly accelerated onto the main road from the alley.

"What is your name?" Trudy asked innocently.

"Taxi driver is my name. Do me the courtesy of not telling me yours," the driver said sharply in Russian.

Trudy nodded and looked at Rod, who just raised his eyebrows in response and then concentrated on their route.

Trudy watched out the window of the cab as they drove through town. Kaunas was a beautiful city with ancient but well-maintained cobblestone streets. The streets were lined with brightly painted brick shops adorned with red tile roofs. The cathedrals and churches were natural-colored brick structures. The town seemed to be completely unaffected by the war, and the bustling street activity gave no hint that the front lines between warring armies were less than one hundred miles away. In a split second, Trudy was jarred back to reality and reminded of her present vulnerability.

"Halt! Papers!" a uniformed man yelled in Lithuanian at the taxi driver as the cab screeched to a halt.

Trudy noticed that the uniforms of the six armed guards at the checkpoint were not the standard German uniforms that she had studied, and she remembered that the SOE briefers had warned her about the Schutzkorps Litauen, the German-controlled Lithuanian soldiers of the Lithuanian Territorial Troops.

The sergeant who appeared to be in charge of the checkpoint examined the driver's papers while two other guards kept weapons trained on Trudy and Rod.

The sergeant returned the driver's papers.

"Turn off your engine, and remain in the car. You two, get out of the car, and hand over your papers," the sergeant yelled at them in Lithuanian.

"Certainly, Sergeant," Trudy said compliantly in German.

"Your papers are Lithuanian, but you are speaking to me in German? Why is that?" the sergeant said with suspicion.

"We are Lithuanian by birth, but we are professors at Freiberg University in Germany. We are here to visit a colleague at Kaunas University," Trudy explained.

"Professor, what do you teach? You are very quiet for a professor. The professors I had normally talked all the time," the sergeant said as he pointed his pistol at Rod.

"I teach history. My colleague in Kaunas has told me about the castle here, and I hope to see it," Rod explained in flawless German.

"And you teach history, too, I imagine. History always bored the shit out of me," the sergeant said with a disgusted look on his face but lowering his pistol to his side.

"Actually, I teach art history, so I am here charged with determining what art needs to be preserved if the Russians get closer. They are already quite close to Vilnius."

"That is a waste of time. The Russians will never take back Lithuania, but I am sure the Germans have paid you well to travel here. Unfortunately, they don't pay us; we get paid by the Lithuanian government."

"Yes, that doesn't seem fair, does it? May I reach into my jacket pocket?" Rod asked.

"Of course, just do it slowly. I am a nervous man," the sergeant said as he raised his pistol once more and pointed it at Rod. The two other guards were still covering them with weapons, too, Rod noticed, and he pulled back the front of his jacket with his left hand before retrieving his wallet with his right hand.

"Slowly," one of the guards now behind Rod yelled.

Rod opened his wallet and pulled out a thick wad of Reichsmarks and peeled off several large bills for the bribe that seemed to be strongly inferred. The sergeant stepped forward to retrieve the bills.

"All right, here are both of your papers," the sergeant said as he returned both Rod's and Trudy's papers to Rod.

"Well, that proves that you are professors. You are a cheap bastard. Anyone else up to no good would have tried to bribe me with way more money. Enjoy your stay in Kaunas," the sergeant said as he returned to the side of the road and waved for the taxi driver to proceed after Trudy and Rod were back in the cab.

"Well done," Trudy complimented Rod.

Rod smiled back at Trudy and then looked out the window of the cab, now worried about more checkpoints.

In less than ten minutes, they were on the campus of Kaunas University. The driver stopped in front of a four-story brick building near the center of the campus.

"I will wait across the street. Take as long as you need. People in a hurry get other people killed," the taxi driver warned.

Rod and Trudy got out and walked up the steep stone steps to the front door of the science building. There was a directory of the professors on the wall. The directory was arranged by floor, and it indicated that Professor Michalonis was in office 202. Rod and Trudy nodded acknowledgment of the room number and headed up the stairs. On the second floor, they noticed that Michalonis's office was the first door on the right. Rod knocked on the door, but there was no answer. A young, voluptuous red-haired woman opened the door across the hall and peered cautiously at Rod and Trudy.

"Professor Michalonis is not here," she said through the crack between the door and wall.

"We are visiting from Vilnius and wanted to say hello to our old friend," Rod lied in Russian.

"Oh, thank God," the woman said as she threw open the door. "I thought you were Gestapo, coming back to search Sammy's office. They took him just a couple of hours ago. I am Professor Viki Stanonis. I do research with Sammy."

"The Gestapo took him?" Trudy said incredulously.

"Yes. They seemed polite and did not hurt him, but they were insistent that he come with them. He told them several times that he had important appointments today related to his research. The walls here are very thin, you know."

"Do you know where they took him?" Trudy asked politely.

"Probably to Gestapo headquarters downtown, but I don't know. I called his wife. She is an English professor and was in class, so she might not have the message yet. Please come in. She should be here soon."

Rod and Trudy followed the professor back into her office, and she looked up and down the hallway before closing the door.

"We all knew that this day would come. The Gestapo knows that Sammy is a Jew, but they have some strange interest in his research, so they have allowed him to continue. It is very unusual," Viki said and then sobbed.

"So, you are friends with his wife, too?" Trudy asked patiently.

"Of course, this is a small university. All the professors know one another by name. Most are close, especially these days. Sonya will be here soon, unless they took her, too," Viki sobbed more and started to cry uncontrollably.

"Can I get you something to drink?" Trudy asked in a very compassionate tone.

"No, that's all right," Viki said as she pulled three water glasses out of her bottom desk drawer and placed them on her desk. She then got up and walked over to a tall filing cabinet and pulled out the V–Z drawer and retrieved a two-thirds-full bottle of vodka.

"You don't have bourbon in the A–B drawer, do you?" Rod quipped.

Viki spit out a laugh through her sobs. "No, just vodka in the V–Z drawer." She laughed finally and stopped crying.

Trudy went over to the window and looked out on the campus. She reached up for the shade and pulled it halfway down so that her face was obscured as she peered out the window from more than a foot back.

Viki stood up and hurried to the window, jerked the shade, and let it retract all the way open again before she looked up and down the street.

"We need sun in here. It is chilly. Is that your car across the street?"

"Yes, our taxi is waiting for us. We paid him extra, and he said that he was not busy today anyhow," Trudy lied before stepping back to the window and resuming her scanning. *It could have been any Midwestern town in the United States*, she thought as she watched two coeds obviously flirting as they walked to class.

Viki stepped back to her desk and poured full glasses of vodka, raised hers, and said "cheers" in English before she downed the glass.

"I know you are not from Vilnius. I just transferred here from there at the beginning of the year. The Gestapo must have known that you were coming. I hope you did not get Sammy killed," Viki lamented.

"We arrived in Vilnius at the beginning of the year, just after you left. We are not science teachers, though. I teach art history, and he teaches German and English," Trudy said as she pointed at Rod and then picked up one of the still full glasses of vodka and took a big gulp. Rod followed her lead and drank a big gulp before he put the glass back on the table. Viki had already started to pour her second glass.

There was a sudden knock on the office door.

"Viki, it's Sonya," a clear voice said from the other side of the door.

Viki jumped up and ran to the door, opened it, and hugged the tall woman with reddish brown hair. Viki held Sonya close with both arms. Sonya hugged her, too, for a moment, and then grabbed Viki by the shoulders and held her at arm's length.

"Viki, what happened? Are you sure that it was the Gestapo who took Sammy?" Sonya asked while completely under control.

"Yes, it was the Gestapo. I saw the car they took him away in. It was one of their big sedans. They also yelled to each other in German as they left the building, so it was not the communists. These two came two hours later, and it scared me half to death since I thought they were Gestapo, too. They say they are from Vilnius, but I am not buying their story," Viki said quickly in Lithuanian to Sonya.

"They are not from Vilnius, but they are friends, so don't ask any more questions, OK?" Sonya replied in Lithuanian. She then seamlessly switched to Russian. "Now, we wait, and either the Gestapo will come here for us all, or they will release Sammy like they have done so many times before. You might as well have a drink while we wait. Viki, do you have another glass for me?"

"I broke the fourth glass last week, so you will need to make do with this teacup," Viki joked.

"Well, fine, but keep the bottle next to the teacup." Sonya forced a smile.

Trudy continued to watch out the window, which had a good view of the street in front of the science building. The taxi driver was still parked across the street, as he had promised.

"Sonya, we have been traveling all day. Could you show me where the bathrooms are located?" Trudy asked.

"Of course, come with me. Do you need to come along, too?" Sonya said, pointing at Rod.

"No, thank you. I am fine for the moment. I will stay here with Viki since she seems distraught," Rod said with a stern look toward Trudy.

"We will be right back," Trudy said cheerfully as she followed Sonya out the door and down the hallway.

Sonya led Trudy to the ladies' room, and once inside, Trudy made sure that it was empty except for her and Sonya. Sonya noticed her checking.

"I thought that you wanted to talk. You are right not to speak freely in front of Viki. I think she is working for the Gestapo, keeping tabs on Sammy."

"What makes you think that?" Trudy asked with a concerned look.

"She arrived at the beginning of the school year and was assigned to help Sammy with his work. For the first couple of months, Sammy complained every day that she knew less about biology than most undergraduate students. Then the complaints stopped, and I got suspicious at the late nights, but soon enough I found out for sure that she was sleeping with him. Her with him? Please excuse my disbelief, but she could have any young man in Kaunas or even a rich general. So far I just sound like a suspicious wife, but I wrote to friends in Vilnius, and they had never heard of her. She also speaks German with a Bavarian accent but says that she learned German in high school. Maybe a school in Munich, but everywhere else teaches High German."

"You may be right. Have you ever noticed that your husband was under surveillance by the Gestapo?"

"No, never, so why would they leave him alone working for them, knowing that he is a Jew? You know they would watch. She is how."

"OK, I do need to pee, and then I will meet you back at her office," Trudy said.

"OK, I went on the way here; remember number 201."

Trudy used the bathroom and inside the stall retrieved the dagger that Rich had given her from her thigh and used the tape to attach it to her left forearm above the sleeve. On the way out of the bathroom, she checked in the mirror to make certain that the knife was not visible.

Trudy entered the office without knocking and watched Viki pour her third glass of vodka.

"*Gruss Gott*," Trudy said casually as she entered the office.

"*Gruss Gott*," Viki replied without thinking, prompting Rod to raise an eyebrow.

"So, what part of Munich did you grow up in?" Trudy asked in German.

Viki turned and walked over to the window, pulling the shade halfway down.

"It is not popular to admit that you have a German father. My mother was Lithuanian, though, and raised me here. Please don't tell the rest of the faculty," Viki pleaded with her back still turned to Trudy.

"Viki, would you pour me another vodka? I think I have room again," Trudy said with a reassuring smile.

"Of course," Viki said as she moved away from the window and walked to her desk to pour Trudy a drink.

Rod looked a bit confused since he had not heard the conversation in the bathroom, but he understood that something was going on, and he moved to the door to block it in case Viki attempted to bolt out or someone else tried to barge in.

Trudy moved to the window and watched as a Mercedes sedan pulled up to the front of the building and a man who looked like he might be Professor Michalonis got out of the back, waved, and headed up the steps in front of the science building. Trudy continued to watch as the car made a U-turn and pulled behind the taxi. Two men in black trench coats got out, one on each side of the car, and approached the taxi from both sides. Trudy saw the puff of exhaust as the taxi motor started. At that point, both men in trench coats pulled PPKs from their coats and pointed them at the driver. They yelled something that Trudy could not hear, and the elderly taxi driver got out of the taxi with his hands up. While this was going on, the professor had arrived on the second floor and was fiddling with his keys to unlock the door of his office. Sonya rushed for the door, and Rod allowed her to greet Sammy in the hallway and bring him into Viki's office.

"The Gestapo just rolled up the taxi driver," Trudy yelled out to Rod in Russian.

Rod rushed over to look, and as he did, one of the Gestapo agents pointed to the window on the second floor after noticing that the shade was halfway down. The man who pointed immediately shot the taxi driver in the head, and he crumpled like a cow at slaughter. The Gestapo agents were now running for the front door.

"Sonya, they are coming. How do we get out of here?" Trudy yelled.

Viki jumped up and pushed past Trudy, pulling up the window and started to yell, "They are..."

Her sentence ended as Rod pushed his commando knife under Viki's rib cage and into her heart.

Sammy tried to rush to Viki's aid, but Sonya grabbed him firmly. "We need to go now. Follow me."

The yell out the window delayed the two Gestapo for just long enough as they tried to listen for further information.

Sonya ran to the opposite end of the hallway and down two flights of stairs into the basement. Leading Sammy, Trudy, and Rod, she weaved through a maze of pipes, boilers, and stacks of boxes. At the far end of the basement, near where steam pipes appeared to go underground, Sonya pulled up a grate and ushered Trudy, Sammy, and Rod down the stairs. Next, Sonya held the grate over her head and went down the narrow metal stairs backward, pulling the grate back into place.

"You look like you have done that before," Trudy said with a very suspicious look.

"I was an undergraduate student here, and we had crazy games and challenges in the steam tunnels. Follow me. I can get us away from them," Sonya said confidently as she pushed past everyone and took the lead. She stopped at the end of all ambient light.

"Keep your head low to avoid pipes overhead. If you hear steam, avoid it. It is hot and dry and will burn the skin off your bones. Hold on to the belt of the person in front of you with one hand, and keep the other hand on the wall for balance in the dark. If you lose your grip, yell out so that I don't leave you. Now, we go," Sonya said.

Sonya slowed at the sound of rustling in front, giving creatures, likely rats that were invisible in the darkness, time to escape the group's approach.

Sonya listened for the sound of the grate behind them but did not hear its distinctive metallic ring over the noise of their feet on the dirt floor. She had learned to avoid that sound as a teenager in college. Sonya stopped suddenly, and everyone ran into the person in front of them with their heads.

"Turning left here," Sonya whispered back to the group. "Is everyone OK?"

"I'm at the back. We are all here," Rod answered.

"OK, let's go. We are almost at the student union. There is a bar there, and it will be crowded. We will go out the side door and head to the botany lab, where Samuel has real friends."

Sonya moved ahead, staying to the left and moving along a curved wall.

"OK, hands and knees here. Do you hear the hissing? That steam will kill you if you stand up. I will stop when we are past the danger."

The group scampered forward on their hands and knees with loud hissing coming over their heads. Trudy felt a small creature scamper across her hand in the direction they had come from and let out a shriek. Rod felt the creature run over his hand, too, and as he reflexively withdrew it, he fell on his left shoulder for a moment and let out all of his air.

Trudy heard the thud and stopped for a moment.

"Don't stand up. Keep going. It is quiet in front of me," Trudy said over the now very loud hissing.

Sonya continued to move ahead, and when she was sure that the last person in the train was past the steam, she stood back up and waited.

Samuel, Trudy, and Rod moved forward on hands and knees and in turn stood up and moved close to Sonya. They could all see light coming from the right up ahead.

"That path to the right leads to the cleaning area in the kitchen of the student union. It will be covered in grease and water, so don't touch the floor, and walk very carefully since it will be slippery. There were always many rats there, too, because of the waste that got washed through the grate. Now, follow me. And no more talking," Sonya instructed.

As they approached the tunnel that went off to the right, it was notice-ably brighter ahead. The floor of the tunnel was also increasingly slippery with a mixture of water and cooking oil. The smell had changed from damp moldy concrete to garbage and rotting meat. Trudy tried not to wretch as she took a full breath of the foul air through her nose. She remembered to suck the air through her teeth instead as her father had taught her when she dressed her first deer. It was still a struggle not to vomit, and the slip-pery floor made falling a real possibility.

Sonya stopped under the grate over her head. Light beamed down on her from above, making her look like some saintly being, as she watched her three companions move down the corridor to the point where they could grasp the metal stair railing.

"OK, I will go first and convince anyone who sees us that we are playing an initiation game. Act very apologetic. These are students working in the kitchen, so don't hurt them, or I will kill you. Do you understand?" Sonya whispered emphatically.

Sonya waited to see Trudy and Rod nod their head in agreement and then headed up the stairs. There was a brief conversation in Lithuanian that Trudy did not understand, and then there was laughter. Sonya ducked into the tunnel and waved for her companions to join her.

As the three others emerged, two college-aged young men laughed heartily. Sammy looked confused by their behavior, but Trudy and Rod smiled at them. Trudy gave a flirtatious wave to an athletic young man as the three followed Sonya single file out the back door of the kitchen and onto a dimly lit loading dock stacked with wooden pallets and empty beer kegs.

Away from the loading dock in a secluded area at the back of the student union, Sonya stopped and motioned everyone to come close.

"Those two were students of mine. I told them that we are all alumni, reliving adventures from undergrad days. They thought that was very hilarious. Here is the problem, though. When the police announce who they are looking for, these boys might say something. They are good boys, and if the police and Gestapo say that they are looking for murderers, any of my students would be likely to say something."

"We have a backup plan to get you out of here, but we need to get to a rowboat hidden near the tip of the peninsula. If we use the boat in broad daylight, someone is bound to see us. There will be no way to escape at that point. Is there anywhere that we could hide until dark without being found?" Rod asked Sonya.

"Maybe. There was an old World War I bomb shelter sealed off after the war. We used to sneak into it, but the university buried the entrance so students would not explore it and go there for mischief," Sonya replied.

"What about stealing a car and driving to the market?" Trudy proposed.

"There are only a few roads out of here; with one of their own dead, the Gestapo will have sealed off the peninsula," Sammy said.

"OK, then, we try to find the World War I bomb shelter, and if we can't, we take the boat during daylight and take our chances. They are going to search this place from one end to the other, and they will find us if we stay," Rod said.

"OK, follow me. We have no time to lose," Sonya said as she started to jog west.

"Whoa, whoa, whoa. Sonya, walk. People notice people running," Trudy advised. "People dressed like us who are running are very suspicious, and people notice. Hold hands with Sammy, and I will hold hands with Rod as we follow you," Trudy directed.

"I didn't expect this to happen," Rod teased Trudy.

"Don't get any ideas. The mission comes first," Trudy said with a slight frown.

Sonya and Sammy led the way. They walked in a seemingly random pattern, and Trudy was becoming suspicious, worried that Sonya was just wasting time until they were caught.

"Here it is," Sonya said as she stomped hard. "Listen to the hollow sound. There is a door here under my feet."

Rod grabbed a metal sign nailed to a tree that showed directions to the river park. He yanked back and forth until it came loose and then ran over to where Sonya was stomping.

Rod used the sign like a shovel and started scraping away the soil as Trudy started looking for another sign to help dig.

As Rod scraped down about three inches, the sound of metal on metal speeded his progress.

"The rains must have washed away most of the dirt that they dumped on top of the door. This high spot is definitely the right place," Sonya said as Rod continued to dig.

"How are we going to hide this? Someone will see the digging and find us," Trudy remarked.

"Sammy, take off your jacket, and fill it with leaves and pine straw over there," Sonya said pointing into a copse of trees.

Sammy followed Sonya's directions while Trudy went over to the same place and scooped up armfuls of leaves and brought them back to where Rod was digging.

The outline of the door was now visible, and Rod used the edge of the sign to pry open the metal trap door. As the door swung open, light filtered on masonry steps descending deep into the ground. There appeared to be water at the bottom of the steps.

The sudden sounds of German shepherd dogs barking startled everyone. Sammy looked at Sonya with horror in his eyes. The dogs were certainly getting closer.

"Let's get down there fast. I'll go down last and pull these branches, leaves, and grass over the door as I lower it. Go down as far as you can without getting wet. If we get wet, we'll die of hypothermia in this cold," Trudy instructed.

Sammy and Sonya went down the steps with the door still open, which allowed them to stop three steps above the level of the water. Rod went down next, and Trudy watched as he sat down several steps above Sammy and Sonya. Rod waved his hand for Trudy to come down.

Trudy slowly lowered the metal door, and with it resting on her shoulders, she pulled the branches and leaves over the opening. The yells of handlers and barks of German shepherds were getting even louder, and Trudy knew that they must be close. As Trudy lowered the door by bending her knees and stepping back down the now pitch-black stairs, all sounds from outside ceased.

Trudy moved slowly now on her hands and knees until she felt Rod. He grabbed onto her and helped steady her until she sat down beside him.

"Now we wait. The problem is I can't read my watch," Rod said.

"Be quiet. The sounds of voices might attract the dogs. Whisper, OK? We can all hear," Trudy said in a whisper.

"I have matches and a watch. It was about two p.m. when we came down here, but it won't get dark enough for us to escape across the river until after six p.m.," Sonya said.

"Why don't you light a cigarette and smoke it? The light from the cigarettes will give us something to look at. This is very disorienting," Sammy complained.

"Maybe later, but we know the dogs are close. And maybe some of the smoke will seep out, and they will find us. We will be really lucky if those are just guard dogs and not trackers. If they have a tracker, they will find us," Sonya explained.

"Why don't you all try and get some sleep? We are going to need it to escape. Just don't fall into the water," Trudy warned.

"I am surprised by the water, but it can't be too deep. There was a sump at the bottom of the stairwell with a small landing before the next set of stairs ascended maybe six or eight feet into a room with brick benches where people would sit and wait for the shelling or bombing to stop," Sonya explained.

"Why would they have a sump? For flooding?" Rod asked.

"No, it was to allow any mustard gas to settle if it seeped in. Mustard gas is heavier than air, so with a sump, they might be able to survive a gas attack, too," Trudy explained.

"Clever," Rod replied.

"OK, someone needs to stay awake, so let's take turns. I'll stay awake first. The rest of you sleep if you can," Trudy offered.

"If we get out of here, you will need to fly. You sleep first, Trudy. I will stay awake," Sonya offered.

"That is very nice of you all, but I can't sleep during the day, and in spite of the darkness, my internal clock is telling me that cocktail hour is just around the corner," said Rod.

"I thought that you might be more concerned about teatime," Trudy quipped.

"Old habits die hard. I never latched on to that Spanish custom of siestas while I was there, either."

"Latch on to any other habits in Spain?" Trudy asked.

"Well, that is where I learned about airplanes even though I only helped the mechanics. I have been fascinated with them ever since," Rod said somewhat circumspectly.

"All right, since no one can sleep, let's make a plan. If the Germans lift up that door, we are all dead," Trudy said.

"Not all of us. They will not kill me, and I will just say that I was kidnapped by American agents," Sammy said proudly.

"Sammy! Why would you even talk that way? What is wrong with you?" Sonya said in a normal tone, forgetting to whisper in her outrage.

"So, Sammy, please tell us. Why did the Gestapo take you away this morning? And a better question, why did they let you go?" Rod said wryly.

"They frequently come and check on me. Sometimes, like today, they take me to their headquarters and question me," Sammy said defensively.

"What questions do they ask?" Trudy asked in a very innocent tone.

"They always ask about my work first. Then they ask about who is helping me and whether anyone is asking about my work. That is all they ever ask," Sammy said with an arrogant tone.

"When I was growing up in New York, some of the kids I knew got mixed up with the mob. Sooner or later, they got arrested. Being a snitch usually got you killed. Keeping your mouth shut meant that you went away to prison for a long time. The police knew this, so they would arrest these guys, take them to the police station, and then charge them with some minor offense that resulted in some small fine. While these guys were at the police station, they would get them to talk about their really bad friends, and if they talked enough, they might even give them some cash to make up for the small fine that they had to pay," Rod said.

"Very interesting story about your criminal friends, but it has nothing to do with me. Maybe you were a criminal, too, with friends like that," Sammy said with disgust.

"The point is nobody who I have ever heard of gets picked up by the Gestapo as often as you do and lives to talk about it. They know you are a Jew. Your research is not completed, so they are not getting any immediate benefits, so why do they spend so much time talking to you? It doesn't make sense to me, and I am risking my life to rescue you," Rod said.

"So, you think that I work for the Gestapo? Fuck you," Sammy said.

"Absolutely. Maybe you don't know it because you have no people skills, and other than science, all you follow is your dick, but reporting to the Gestapo on a regular basis means that you work for them," Rod said with a disgusted tone.

"What I am doing is so important that any government would kiss my ass to learn about it. There is a code that makes each of us different. When we learn to modify that code, we can change the very nature of humans. We can eliminate disease. We can make every man a genius. We can make every man an athlete," Sammy said loudly.

"Or we can make every man a perfect blond-haired and blue-eyed warrior. You know that is what they want you for. You are a black-haired, brown-eyed Jew who has betrayed your people just like Dimitri said," Trudy said with disgust.

"Well, fuck you. I said that I would not leave with the English partisans and that I wanted the Americans to come get me to work with Albert Einstein. Well, fuck you all. I am not going anywhere," Sammy announced.

"Sammy, you are so worked up. You don't really want to work for the Nazis. We will be out of here soon, and you will be able to work with other geniuses like you. Albert Einstein will be proud to work with you. You know that," Sonya said soothingly.

"I feel so afraid. I must have light soon. Please comfort me," Sammy whispered to Sonya.

"Wow, what a mess. Do you think that he is even worth saving?" Trudy whispered in Rod's ear.

"OSS and SOE think so. We are here, so I don't care if he wants to go or not; we are putting his ass in my airplane," Rod whispered back.

"We certainly are. Sonya certainly seems key to keeping him in a cooperative mood. I think that she has figured out that he is some kind of socially disconnected sex maniac. She was probably relieved that he was sleeping with that Nazi bitch," Trudy whispered.

"So, what happens now?" Trudy asked Rod.

"Well, I'm not going to sleep, so let's see how deep that water is and find out if there is at least another place to hide in case someone surprises us and opens the door," Rod whispered back.

"Sonya, when you finish whatever it is you are doing with Sammy, we need you to light a match and see how deep the water is, OK?" Trudy said in a normal voice.

After a pause, Sammy let out a low moan, and Trudy could hear clothing being adjusted.

"Oh, boy," Rod commented.

"I am looking for the matches. Yes, I have them, but it feels like there are only five or maybe six left in the package," Sonya said as she lit the first match and peered across the water at the bottom of the stairs. "This water is crystal clear. It looks good enough to drink," Sonya said as the first match burned out. "The level of the water is just below the ceiling of the corridor into the shelter," she said.

"Well, now we know why we haven't all started getting drowsy from carbon-dioxide poisoning. There is a lot more space for air than I thought. Could we make it into the shelter if we were willing to get wet? Maybe one of us should get undressed and check it out?" Trudy asked.

"That would be a very bad idea. Right now we have drinking water. As much as I would like to see you with your clothes off, if you go into the water, you will stir up any silt on the bottom, and we will not be able to drink it. Right now we have a source of water and will not die of thirst if we need to stay in here another day," Sammy said.

"How do you know it's drinkable?" Rod asked.

"It is just like a cave where the water percolates through limestone and is filtered. In this case the water has seeped through the thick cement and maybe some tiny cracks. I am a biologist, remember," Sammy reminded them.

"OK, genius, there is one problem with your logic. If any of us urinates, where do you think that it will go?" Rod asked.

"Yes, you are right, but it would be diluted enough that it would still be OK to drink if you were dying. It is disgusting to think about, though," Sammy admitted.

"In that case, I suggest anyone who needs a drink to get it now because I need to take a piss really soon," Rod admitted.

"You are talking like we are going to be in here for days. Jonas and Dimitri will not wait for us after tomorrow night, and every hour we spend in here, there is an even greater chance that your airplanes will be discovered," Sonya said.

"Wait a minute. How do you know about Dimitri and Jonas? I do remember Dimitri saying last night that he had met Sammy, but I never told you that they brought us into Kaunas," Trudy said suspiciously.

"They actually work for me," Sonya said.

"Not teaching English, I take it. This explains a lot. And you knew about this, Sammy?" Rod asked pointedly.

"Of course I knew about this, and I didn't tell the Gestapo about it or else Sonya wouldn't be sitting here with us right now. You are such a putz," Sammy said.

"That explains how the SOE was so certain that this wasn't a trap and that you were worth retrieving. So, how long have you worked for them?" Trudy asked.

"Just ask her where she went to school. With her accent it was likely Cambridge or Oxford. No doubt they recruited her there," Rod announced.

"Speculate all you want. Where did they recruit you? You seem to know so much about how they do business," Sonya shot back at him.

"Sonya, did you come right back here after school?" Trudy asked.

"No, I spent a year in Malmo, Sweden, first. The British have a very quiet relationship with Sweden. Even though Sweden is supposed to be neutral, there is a large British presence in Malmo that supports the air war in some way that I don't fully understand. I taught Swedes English so that they could work with the English in Malmo.

"Stop, enough of this. You stupid spies are giving me a headache," Sammy said in a mournful tone.

"OK, last call if you want water. I am coming down to the bottom of the stairs and taking a leak," Rod said as he moved past Trudy and slowly descended the steps, careful not to step on Sonya or Sammy and well aware that there were only three steps past them before he would step into the water. "Last chance," Rod warned as the sound of a zipper was heard. Five seconds later, the sound of splashing water went on for almost a minute.

"Wow, you really had to go," Sonya joked.

"I'm a pilot. I am used to holding it for a long time."

"That was a good idea. I am not a pilot, but I need to go now, too," Sammy said as the sound of another zipper going down was heard.

"Lucky for us, Sonya showed me the way to the bathroom back at the science building," Trudy joked.

The group was quiet again after Rod made his way back up the steps and reclaimed his perch next to Trudy.

"I might be able to sleep now," Rod said as he leaned against the wall.

"Just don't fall down the stairs. I don't think either Sammy or Sonya can fly your plane, unless Sonya has another surprise," Trudy said, only half joking.

"No, I am not a pilot, and Sammy has never been in an airplane," Sonya said before she let out a long yawn.

At least another hour went by. It was hard to tell with no change in the light that would indicate the end of another day.

"Should we check up above? I think that we need some fresh air in here anyhow," Trudy said out loud.

"You will also let the cold in," Sammy complained.

"So, do you want to stay in here forever?" Trudy replied back.

"No, of course I don't. Do what you want."

"Rod? Do you want to give me a hand? Are you asleep?" Trudy nudged him.

"I guess I drifted off. Maybe we had better let some fresh air in here. I am getting a bit of a headache, too," Rod said as he moved up the stairs on hands and knees but still managed to bump his head on the steel door at the top. "Ouch, that hurt."

Rod bowed his head and used his shoulders and legs to push the door open a crack and listen. There were no sounds of barking dogs or soldiers yelling directions. It was also dark, so they had misjudged the time that they had been underground. Rod cautiously moved a little bit higher and pushed the door open a few inches more. The cold air hugging the ground poured into the shelter like water going over a falls, and Rod's three companions all shivered as the cold air hit them, too. Rod peered out in three directions, and all was clear. He was unable to check in the direction of the door hinges, so he listened for a few seconds longer. No sounds of footsteps. All seemed quiet. Rod pushed the door open more and poked his head out of the shelter. There was a flashlight swinging back and forth on a trail several hundred yards away, but the owner of the flashlight was going in the other direction. Rod let the door close and faced down the steps.

"OK, there was one person with a flashlight going in the opposite direction a few hundred yards away. It is completely dark, so let's get out of here. No talking after I open the door. Sammy, are you with us or staying?"

"I am with you," Sammy said in a weary tone.

"Sonya, when you get outside, we will follow you to the boat. We have rough directions, but I take it you know exactly where it is?" Rod asked.

"Yes, of course I do. I helped hide it," Sonya responded.

"OK, let's go," Rod said as he opened the door cautiously a second time, carefully peering out in three directions once more before he climbed out and lowered the door into the fully open position.

The others climbed out of the shelter. Sammy hunched over like he was hiding.

"Stand up straight like you belong here," Rod whispered in Sammy's ear, and Sammy looked surprised but nodded and stood up straight as he looked in all directions. Sonya motioned and headed through the woods toward the river.

I hope they didn't find the boat while they were looking for us, Trudy thought as she followed Sammy, who was staying close to Sonya. Rod took up the rear and glanced over his shoulder, watching to make sure that they would not be surprised from behind. Sonya stopped at the sound of a motorboat out on the river and froze in place as a floodlight from the boat swept across the riverbank in front of them in a random pattern. The boat continued at a steady speed, and the random pattern with the searchlight continued as the boat moved upriver and focused its search on the base of the bridge into Kaunas.

Sonya waved for them to follow as she started walking toward the riverbank again and into heavier brush.

"Come help. We buried it upside down so the bottom of the boat is level with the ground. It will take all of us to get it out of the hole. Grab onto these ropes on the downhill side, and pull up. We can drag it over the edge of the hole that way and then flip it over after we get it out of the hole."

Trudy, Rod, and Sammy pulled the boat out of the hole and flipped it over while Sonya pushed from the other side and then jumped into the hole to retrieve the two oars and laid them inside the boat before the others started dragging it toward the river.

"We had better mount the oars before we get it in the water," Trudy cautioned, having been around boats all of her life.

Rod worked on the one on the port side while Trudy worked on starboard.

"This is going to be a tight fit for four people," Rod whispered to Sonya. "Can he swim?" Rod said, pointing at Sammy.

"Why are you asking her? Yes, I can swim, just not very well. Let's go," Sammy said as he helped push the boat into the water and jumped in.

"I'll row," Rod offered.

"That works for me," Trudy whispered back, and she climbed into the boat next.

Sonya was the lightest, so she waited until Trudy, Rod, and Sammy were all seated and then she pushed the bow of the boat off land and jumped in.

"Shit! I just got a shoe full of water," Sonya complained as she seated herself, and Rod turned the boat with the oars.

Trudy looked up and down the river for any sign of the motorboat with the searchlight. It couldn't be close since the only sound they could hear were the oars smoothly going in and out of the water with a faint *kerplunk* sound.

He seems to know what he is doing since he isn't splashing, Trudy thought.

Rod angled the boat downstream at a forty-five-degree angle to the bank and headed the rowboat toward the left bank just past where the Neris joined the Neman. The rest of the group watched and listened for any signs of trouble. They all understood how vulnerable they were in the rowboat.

Trudy heard it first and turned to look behind them. The distinct sound of the motorboat was getting louder by the second as it headed toward them still around a bend in the river. Rod pulled hard on the oars and angled more sharply toward the shore. The boat was now visible as it came around the bend in the river but still more than a quarter of a mile away. Rod pulled harder and beached the front of the boat on the river-bank, making a slight scrapping sound as the bow slid across sand and gravel.

Sonya jumped out and held the bow of the boat as Rod, then Trudy, and then Sammy climbed across the bow, managing to keep their feet dry. Sammy grabbed the gunnels near the bow and pulled while Rod mirrored his actions on the other side of the boat.

"If they look closely, they will be able to see where we dragged the boat into the bushes," Trudy said.

"Looks like they stopped right about where we got in. I wonder if they saw our footprints on the riverbank," Rod said.

"They must have. Now they are focusing the spotlight right where the boat was hidden," Sonya said. "Come on, follow me. Hopefully Jonas and Dimitri are still waiting. It won't take the Gestapo long to figure out where we hid the boat on this side of the river."

As they climbed up the brush-covered riverbank, the silhouette of a man who looked like Dimitri put up his hand and motioned Sonya to stop, and then he started waving for them to get down. When Dimitri was sure that they were staying put on the ground, he crawled to them below the level of the brush tops on his hands and knees. Rod had his knife out, holding it in his right hand while he stayed motionless on his hands and knees like a big cat ready to pounce on its prey. He recognized Dimitri and strained to hear what he and Sonya were whispering, but he could not make out the words. Dimitri turned and watched in the direction he had crawled from while Sonya crawled back to inform everyone what was going on.

"Jonas was stopped by the side of the road in his wagon while Dimitri came into the woods to wait for us. Two German soldiers drove up in a Kubelwagon and started asking questions, so Jonas tried to bribe them with some vodka. Now the three of them are standing around getting drunk, and they don't seem to want to leave. I told Dimitri that the Gestapo will soon figure out where we beached the boat and will send patrols over here."

"If they talk to these two soldiers, they will know that Jonas was here waiting. We need to kill these guys now," Rod whispered insistently.

"Trudy, are you as good at combatives as Donovan said you were?" Rod asked.

"Better, actually. I was first in my class," Trudy whispered with a smile.

"OK, we wait until their backs are turned, and we rush them. You grab one, and I will grab the other, but you will need to hold yours for a moment while I stab the guy I grab and then stab the fellow whom you are holding."

"I appreciate your offer of help, and maybe I will need it if these guys are particularly big, but I have a knife, too," Trudy said as she ripped off the tape from her arm that held her dagger and showed it to Rod, who smiled and waved for her to follow him as they crawled to Dimitri. They explained to Dimitri what their plan was.

"I don't like it. If you get hurt and can't fly, you will be stuck here," Dimitri cautioned.

"We both understand that, but if we don't get out of here fast, we will both be dead anyhow," Trudy whispered to Dimitri.

"OK, you try it your way, but I will watch with my pistol. I won't let Jonas or either of you get killed. I will use the gun if I must, but any shots and the garrison at the bridge downstream will come to investigate. And we may all be caught."

"We are wasting time. Let's go, Trudy," Rod said as he crawled toward the road. Trudy moved in a low crouch, unable to crawl anymore on her very scratched-up bare knees.

As Rod arrived at the top of the gently sloping riverbed, he could hear men speaking in German and laughing. As he looked out of the bushes and saw Jonas drinking with the two Germans, he noticed that Jonas was facing the two Germans who had their backs to the river and were watching up and down the road, probably concerned that a superior would catch them stopped and drinking vodka while they were supposed to be patrolling.

Rod waved at Jonas, and Jonas pulled another bottle of vodka off the cart, opened it, took a long swig, and handed it to the German on Trudy's left. Rod whispered very quietly in her ear. "When the next guy tilts his head back to drink, take him out, and I will take out the guy who just drank."

Trudy watched the first German hand the bottle to the second, who stood for a moment holding the bottle, and asked his buddy what time it was before putting the bottle up to his mouth. Trudy sprung forward like a lioness, and while the German was still swallowing, Trudy grabbed his head, pulled it back, and drove the dagger deep into the soldier's throat. Simultaneously, Rod grabbed the other German soldier, who was for a moment also distracted as he tried to pull back his jacket sleeve to see his wristwatch. Rod pulled him back by the forehead and dragged his commando knife across the soldier's throat, literally cutting him from ear to ear. Jonas was already moving forward to make sure that the soldier who Trudy had attacked was completely dead.

Dimitri waved to Sonya, who stood up and walked up the slope with Sammy.

"Jonas and Dimitri, put the Germans in the back seat of the Kubelwagon. Then get going toward your place in the cart. I'll drive the car with Rod, Sammy, and Trudy. Rod, you and Sammy get to sit on the bodies."

"OK, let's go," Trudy said as she helped arrange the bodies in the back of the German military jeep and positioned herself in the front passenger seat. Jonas and Dimitri were already headed down the road in the horse-drawn cart.

"The Germans might let them go if they stop them. The three of us look a mess. Between the blood, mud, scratches, and torn-up knees, they would take us in for sure, even if they didn't recognize Sammy," Sonya said as she started the Kubelwagon and put it in gear.

"If anyone tries to stop us, just drive as fast as you can," Rod advised.

"I am already driving as fast as I can in the dark with the lights out. This thing normally only holds two, and we have six in here now. It is bottoming out on every bump."

"It's still faster than the horse-drawn cart and a lot more comfortable than hiding in the hidden compartment," Trudy reminded Rod.

"Our best bet is to pull off the road and take off on foot if they spot us. This thing is not built for speed. If we run into a Gestapo sedan, we won't have any chance of getting away on the road.

"What are we going to do with the bodies?" Rod asked.

"We will sink them in the swamp. While you are back there, get their guns. One of them had a Luger; I saw the MP-40, which must have belonged to the other one. Check his belt for spare magazines; they usually carry at least three extra in a leather case on their belt."

"Ah, you are right; we have three more that feel like they are full. That makes our chances a little bit better," Rod said as he checked to make sure that the MP-40 Schmeiser submachine gun had rounds in the magazine and the bolt was locked back. He checked the Luger, too, and then handed it to Trudy.

Sammy felt left out and complained. "Why didn't you give the gun to me? She already has a knife and seems to know how to use it."

"Because you aren't a trained soldier, and she has been shooting most of her life. You can have the next one we take," Rod reassured him.

"I hope that we will not need to take another one, especially this close to Dimitri's home. They would rip it apart looking for partisans," Sammy said with a surprisingly compassionate tone.

"We should be there in another fifteen minutes. How soon do you want to fly out of here?" Trudy asked Rod.

"I would prefer waiting until maybe an hour before sunrise, but we will need to discuss this with Jonas and Dimitri," Rod replied.

"I think you should get us the hell out of here as soon as possible," Sonya said between the bone-jarring potholes.

"We need to get you both into warmer clothing; otherwise, you will freeze to death up at altitude. Dimitri told us that he has taken care of that," Trudy warned.

"OK, in that case, we go to the farmhouse first and wait for Dimitri and Jonas. You two can get a little bit of sleep before we take off," Sonya recommended.

"Still no car lights. That is a good sign," Trudy commented.

Sonya made a sharp right turn onto a single-lane road. Up ahead, Trudy could see the silhouette of the barns where the two Mustangs were hidden. Sonya slowed down as she turned again onto the single-lane tractor path through the trees that they had followed from the barn to the farmhouse.

"Sonya, stop. Don't drive this to the farmhouse. We want Angie to be able to say that she has never seen it. Pull it into the barn, and we will walk the rest of the way," Trudy urged.

"That's as good idea," Sonya said as she shifted the Kubelwagon in reverse and pulled back onto the single-lane dirt road that led to the barns.

"This will hide it from the air, too. Good idea, Trudy," Rod agreed.

Sonya maneuvered the vehicle into the barn.

"Wow, I can't believe we made it," Trudy said as a short smile emerged.

"We are not out of here yet," Rod said.

"How much longer do you think it will take Dimitri and Jonas to get here?" Trudy asked Sonya.

"At least another hour. We were probably only going about twice as fast since I was driving with the lights out. They are probably pushing the horse more than normal so maybe less than an hour."

"Let's use the time to get the canvas off the planes. We will be flying out of here before light anyhow," Rod advised.

"OK, show us what to do," Sammy agreed, and Sonya nodded.

"This is going to be really hard. The canvas will be stiff as hell since it is so cold out," Trudy noted as she remembered a winter hunting trip with her father.

"Let's lower one side completely and then roll the canvas toward the other side. When we get the two pieces on top of the airplanes, we will lower the other side and lift the roll off the wing," Rod said as he looked over the position of the canvas.

"Just be careful of the propeller," Trudy warned.

"I think we can lower it behind the propeller if you and Sonya get on the wings and pull it back while Sammy and I lower it."

"OK, we are on it," Trudy said as she showed Sonya where and where not to step on the wing.

The planning paid off, and the canvas was removed from both airplanes within thirty minutes.

"We need to roll this canvas all the way up and use the rope to tie it, or it will catch our prop wash when we start the engines," Trudy said as she stretched out a corner of the piece of canvas closest to her. Sonya and Rod pitched in while Sammy watched after complaining that his hands hurt from the cold.

As the group finished rolling up the second piece of canvas, they noticed the sound of a trotting horse and the squeaks from the cart on the rough road.

"They're here," Trudy declared as she rushed around the side of the barn, only pausing to pick up the MP-40 in case it was not Jonas and Dimitri.

Rod ran around the other side of the barn in case this turned into a firefight. As he emerged, he watched as Trudy greeted Jonas and Dimitri. Rod walked over to join them.

"Trudy, Jonas will take care of the horse and cart. We will get the others and head up to the house. Angie will have some stew or goulash ready. I know everyone must be hungry. I have the warm clothes that Sonya and Sammy will need, and we can stand guard while you and Rod get a few hours of sleep," Dimitri said.

After the short walk to the farmhouse, they gathered around the table recounting their action-filled day to Angie as she brought several bowls of a chicken-based cabbage stew to the table. The hot food did wonders for their spirits, and as they relaxed, the stress from their adventures caught up with them. Trudy could barely keep from falling asleep, and she noted that Rod was also starting to nod off.

"Dimitri, please don't let us sleep past five. I am going to lay out my flight gear and get at least a couple hours of sleep so that I can fly," Trudy said as she got up from the table. "The food was wonderful, Angie. Thank you so much."

Angie smiled and came over and gave Trudy a hug. "You are most welcome. Angels will protect you while you sleep," Angie said with a smile and nodded toward Dimitri.

Trudy headed up the stairs and started organizing her flight gear by the light of the kerosene lamp by the bed. Rod knocked on the door to announce that he was coming in and started the same process of laying out his gear on the floor on his side of the bed.

While Rod was straightening things out on the floor, Trudy pulled off her clothing and, as she sat on the edge of the bed, stripped naked and slid under the covers. Rod hadn't noticed Trudy undressing. He went through the same routine of taking off his clothes as he had the night before and then turned down the lamp before crawling under the covers, too, and lay on his side with his back to Trudy.

"It seems colder in here tonight," Rod complained wearily.

"Then come closer. I'm chilled, too.

Rod rolled onto his back and moved next to Trudy and was surprised to feel her naked body next to his, expecting her to be sleeping in her flight suit again.

"Come here, and get warm," Trudy said as she placed her arm across Rod's chest, and the two became entwined in a warm embrace. Rod moved on top of Trudy, and they made love until it seemed like all their remaining energy was drained. Rod rolled back over onto his back. Trudy rested her head on his chest and kissed Rod's neck, and he continued to hold her close. And she realized that he had already fallen asleep. Trudy relaxed and fell asleep in Rod's arms.

When Trudy awoke several hours later, Rod was gently brushing her hair back from her eyes. "Didn't you hear Dimitri knocking?" Rod whispered as Trudy slowly woke up.

"No, is it five?"

"Almost. Are you ready for some flying?"

"Yes, but let's take care of something else first," Trudy said as she reached down below Rod's waist. "Lie on your back this time," Trudy whispered back as she rolled over on top of Rod.

Trudy and Rod made love the second time and were catching their breath when there was another knock.

"It is almost five thirty. It will be light soon," Dimitri advised.

"We are almost ready," Trudy lied as she jumped out of bed, once again full of energy, and began getting into her flight gear. Rod did the same, and the two dressed facing each other and smiling as they prepared for the long flight ahead.

In another ten minutes, they were headed down the stairs. There was milk, sausage, and fried potatoes on the table with plates stacked next to them. Sammy and Sonya were just finishing their food. Angie came into the room.

"Please help yourself. I knew you would be in a hurry, and I wasn't sure if you ate before flying."

"This is perfect," Trudy said as she spooned some of the potatoes onto a plate and savored a few sips of the fresh, cold milk.

"Dimitri and Jonas are taking care of the dead Germans. We should get going in case they run into any trouble. I woke up with a funny feeling about today, and I am a little worried."

"Always trust your intuition, Sonya," Angie advised.

"I normally do, and it has served me well. We were certainly more than lucky yesterday," Sonya said as she gave a farewell hug to Angie.

"Good luck to all of you. Come back when the war is over," Angie invited.

"I will make a point of doing that," Trudy said as she, too, gave Angie a hug and headed out the door. They started the short walk to the barns with their breath billowing vapor.

"Sonya, you will ride in Trudy's Mustang, and Sammy will ride in mine. When we get to the planes, we will get you both strapped in, and then Trudy and I will go through our preflight check and start-up procedures. OK?"

Sonya and Sammy both nodded in agreement, and when they arrived at the airplanes, getting the two on board went as planned with both Sammy and Sonya following their pilot's directions to the letter. Trudy and Rod went through their checks, and Rod was the first to start his airplane and performed an intercom check with Sammy.

"Sammy, I need to get out and remove the wheel chocks. Stay put, OK?"

"Not a problem. I am fine," Sammy said with excitement, looking forward to his first flight.

Rod climbed out of the cockpit and headed over to Trudy's Mustang. He pulled the Colt M-1911 pistol out of his shoulder holster, cocked the weapon, and dangerously placed it in his right front pants pocket without setting the safety before he climbed up onto the wing of Trudy's Mustang. Trudy was surprised to see Rod on the wing of her airplane since she was just about to start her engine.

"What's up?" Trudy yelled over the rumble and prop wash of Rod's Mustang.

"Slight change of plans, Trudy. We won't be flying back to England today."

"What?" Trudy said incredulously.

"Sammy is going with me to Russia," Rod said in a matter-of-fact tone.

Trudy switched on the intercom so that Sonya could hear what she was saying and slowly started to reach for the single-shot .45 that was in her outer pants pocket.

"So, was this the SOE plan all along? Do you have some kind of a deal worked out with the Russians?"

"Fuck the SOE. This is about doing what is right for me," Rod declared. "Now, keep your hands where I can see them while we go over this. The Russians will send you back to America after the war. They are beating the Germans now, so you will be perfectly safe in Moscow instead of going on another foolhardy mission for General Donovan."

"Rod, I'm not taking Sonya to Russia and letting the NKVD torture her until they find all the SOE in the Baltics, and I am not going to allow you to take Sammy there, either," Trudy declared.

"First, let's take this SOE whore out of the equation," Rod yelled, and without warning he held his Colt M-1911 to Sonya's temple and pulled the trigger. She died instantly as a fog of blood covered the other wing of the airplane.

Trudy felt cold rage. Hours ago she had made love to this murderer, and she reached for the M-1911 in her shoulder holster. Rod had the advantage since Trudy was still strapped in, and he now pointed the gun at Trudy's head.

"Don't do that. I don't want to kill you. I have actually grown quite accustomed to having you around over the last several months. The Russians will make us comfortable, even after the war is over."

"Are you completely insane? You are an American army officer. You are a traitor, and they will hunt you down and hang you. So, this had nothing to do with the SOE? I thought that you were still working for them."

"Oh, I was recruited by SOE while I was in the hospital, just as General Donovan suspected. The funny thing is I had already been recruited by the NKVD while I was in Spain. While Hitler was arming the Fascists, Russia was arming the Republicans and sending advisers. I was already working for the NKVD when the SOE pitched me to join them. I agreed to work for the SOE to take revenge on those bastards. Our dear Lord Mountbatten got a lot of good men killed when he lobbied politicians to override the saner members of the Ministry of Defense and carry out the Dieppe mission. Then Mountbatten was rewarded with command of the Southeast Asian theater for his failed slaughter of good men on both sides."

"So, this isn't about doing what is right; this is about personal revenge," Trudy yelled at Rod bitterly.

"Call it what you may. The fact is that SOE will not be bragging about a miraculous rescue that they can use to lobby for even greater power. This will be a failure that they will pay a heavy price for politically."

"There is no way in hell that I am going to follow you to Russia. I'm taking Sonya to England and making sure that she is buried like the hero that she is," Trudy said with rage still in her voice and watching for an opportunity to start the engine and knock Rod off the wing.

"Trudy, I am not going to leave you with a choice," Rod said as he pointed his pistol at the wing he was standing on and pulled the trigger. The bullet passed through the wing, and there was a strong smell of aviation gasoline as the fuel spilled out of the wing. Trudy expected him to fire the weapon again and ignite the fuel, and she started to grab for her harness in a panic.

"Stop!" Rod said firmly as he held the gun back to Trudy's head. "Now, slowly reach down and shut off the wing tank so that you don't lose all your fuel. The wing tank will empty out, and you will have enough fuel to make it to Russian lines, but you will never make it back to England now. So, here is what happens next. I am going to get into my airplane and fly

Sammy to Moscow, and I suggest you follow me. If you run out of fuel before you make it all the way, set down at an airfield or on a road. I will make sure they are expecting you. I'll see you in Moscow," Rod said as he jumped off the wing and ran to his airplane.

Trudy unstrapped and jumped onto the wing of her airplane; she reached in to check for signs of life from Sonya and found the entire side of Sonya's head missing opposite the entry wound. Trudy gagged and vomited. She reached for her pistol while she was still doubled over and aimed at Rod's plane with the M-1911 and fired all seven rounds at the airplane as it taxied away with no obvious sign that she had damaged the aircraft.

Jonas came around the corner as she was firing her weapon. Not knowing what was going on, he pointed the MP-40 at Trudy and moved forward, noting that the slide of the M-1911 was locked open, indicating that it was empty.

"What happened?" Jonas demanded.

"Rod shot Sonya and is taking Sammy to Russia," Trudy yelled back at him. "I have got to stop him!"

"Kill him, Trudy. Sammy must not end up in Russia after all Sonya has sacrificed. Your airplane is leaking fuel, though."

"I know, but I have enough in the other two tanks to stop him," Trudy said as she jumped into the cockpit and began the start-up sequence. "Get away from the plane," Trudy yelled as she waved her arm for Jonas to get back.

The whine of the starter was replaced with the deafening roar of the Mustang's engine, and Trudy released the brakes and taxied forward. She felt urgency to go fast but stayed calm enough to keep her taxi speed slow enough to make the sharp turn around the barn. Rod was already at the end of the runway preparing to make the short field takeoff by holding the brakes and increasing the throttle to full power before releasing the brakes and catapulting down the runway. Trudy watched Rod fly off as she taxied to the end of the runway and decided to perform a riskier rolling start, judging that she had enough runway, and the air was cold and dense.

As Trudy made the turn onto the small airstrip, she pushed the throttle forward as soon as she knew that she was lined up properly. Trudy had not anticipated the extra drag from the rolling resistance of her landing gear on the dirt runway, and she had barely achieved takeoff speed at the end of the runway. Trudy was airborne now, but she barely missed the line of trees and for a moment lost track of where Rod had gone.

With her landing gear and flaps retracted, the Mustang was soon at near top speed as she chased Rod, noting that he was flying due east. Trudy armed her guns and fired a one-second burst to make sure the two M-2 Brownings were functioning.

Trudy was slowly gaining on Rod as she flew well above the more fuel-efficient cruising speed that Rod maintained. Trudy noticed that there was a line of BF-109 Messerschmitt and FW-190 fighters evenly disbursed along an airfield between Kaunas and Vilnius. She hoped that the German fighters would stay on the ground as she passed their base now heading into Russia.

Within ten minutes, Trudy was on Rod's tail and was almost within machine-gun range. As Trudy was almost ready to pull the trigger, Rod made a rapid left-hand banking maneuver, and she no longer had a shot.

"I guess we don't need to worry about radio silence anymore." Rod's voice crackled over the radio. "Maintain your current heading, and fly in front of me, or I will shoot you down. I think that might be what you were intending to do to me a few seconds ago."

"You had better tell Sammy that you are about to get him killed, you bastard," Trudy replied over the radio as she went to full power and pushed the stick forward, forcing the Mustang into a steep diving turn. Rod had not expected the maneuver, and as he attempted to follow Trudy, he realized that she was inside his turning radius due to her earlier maximum G turn.

Without warning, Trudy pulled up and cut power for a moment to create the normally undesirable left-wing stall. She then watched as Rod shot past her and first turned one direction and then the other, having lost track of Trudy.

"That was your last chance, Trudy. I am afraid that I will have to shoot you down now," Rod said over the radio.

"Burn in hell," Trudy replied as she went to full power and pulled back on the stick to place Rod in front of her as she fired her two M-2s and watched the tracer rounds stream toward Rod's Mustang in the three seconds that she could keep him in front of her. Trudy watched as pieces flew off of Rod's left wing, and he banked left and dived to get out of the line of fire.

As Rod tried to bring the wings back to a level position, he felt the sluggishness of what should have been a sharp maneuver, and he realized that most of the left aileron was missing and he was streaming fuel from the left-wing tank. Trudy's superior dogfighting skills enraged Rod, and he applied full power and attempted to fly low over the rolling countryside to evade Trudy, but giving in to his rage, he turned and climbed in an attempt to reengage in the dogfight and defeat her.

Trudy was already higher than Rod by a few hundred feet, and when he attempted another sluggish turn in his damaged airplane, Trudy turned inside and unleashed another three-second burst with her machine guns into Rod's path. She stayed behind, now matching Rod's speed as he turned into the stream of bullets, and black smoke erupted from his engine. Rod started losing altitude almost immediately, and Trudy watched as he attempted to line up with a dirt road for an emergency landing. As he attempted to make the turn to line up, the tendency of the aircraft to left-wing stall at low speed revisited itself upon Rod, and Trudy watched with satisfaction as the Mustang struck the ground with its left wing and then nose before it cartwheeled across an open field and came to rest in a crumpled heap.

Trudy made a low passing turn and tried to check for signs of life, but she saw none. She flew past the crash site and made a long sweeping turn as she climbed and lined up for a gun run on the wreckage. At seven hundred feet above the terrain, Trudy placed the wreckage in her sight and squeezed the trigger, unleashing a torrent of bullets. The white phosphorus tracers were still burning at such close range. And the bullets with their fiery tails ignited the fuel, and the wreck exploded into a ball of flame and a tower of black smoke. Trudy made one more pass to convince herself that nobody could have survived the inferno.

"Like I said, Rod, burn in hell," Trudy said over the radio.

Now convinced that both Sammy and Rod were dead, she turned to fly in the direction of England and began climbing to her cruising altitude.

As Trudy climbed past six thousand feet, she realized that she was still streaming fuel from her right wing, which should have drained long ago.

Trudy checked her gauges once more and was alarmed that the hole in the wing was now draining fuel from all of her tanks. Her attempt to isolate the tank had been unsuccessful, and Trudy guessed that the bullet Rod fired into the tank had unintentionally also damaged the valve that could have isolated the leaking tank from the tank in the fuselage and the other wing tank.

At her current rate of fuel consumption and loss from the hole in the wing, Trudy estimated that she had maybe twenty minutes of fuel left, which might get her to the coast. She thought for a moment about heading back into Russia, but she knew that even the earlier versions of the Mustangs had not been provided to Russia under Lend Lease and she was not going to give a potential future adversary access to the Mustang's cutting-edge technology.

Trudy leveled off at six thousand feet and turned back toward Kaunas. She remembered the disbursed German fighters scattered along the length of both sides of the military airstrip and wondered if they were kept fueled, which seemed to be standard practice in most militaries. Trudy knew that the Germans were experiencing fuel shortages and also wondered if that is why they had not taken off to intercept her when she flew overhead at full power as she chased Rod into Russia. If she returned to that airfield now, she would be high enough that they might not notice the sound of her engine, and anyhow, they would be unlikely to scramble fighters to chase after a lone enemy fighter.

Trudy remembered that her pistol was empty after firing all seven rounds at Rod's plane, and she pulled one of the two spare magazines out of the holder attached to her shoulder holster. Trudy held the stick between her knees, and, holding the pistol in her right hand, she pressed the magazine release and dropped the empty magazine into her lap. With her left hand, Trudy slammed the spare magazine into the pistol and then hit the slide release with her thumb, which let the slide go forward and pushed a live round into the chamber. The hammer was still at full cock, and Trudy applied the thumb safety before she placed the M-1911 pistol back in her shoulder holster.

Trudy also double checked the flare pistol in the survival pouch on the side of the cockpit since she had never fired one of the flare pistols before.

Trudy refocused her attention on flying now, still cognizant of the rapid fuel loss. Trudy could see Vilnius off her left wing now, and she knew that the German fighter base would also be on her left before she passed Kaunas. She continued to fly straight and level as she could see the base in front of her now between her left wing and propeller. There seemed to be an unusual absence of activity at the base with a few cars and service trucks moving around but no sign of activity near the airplanes. Trudy passed the base and was almost past Kaunas when she started to descend. She thought for a moment about trying to make it to the Baltic Sea, but some quick calculations convinced her that she would be miles short of the coast, and her fuel tanks would be completely empty, preventing her from ensuring the destruction of the valuable aircraft.

Trudy made her decision, and once she was about twenty miles west of Kaunas, she made a one-hundred-eighty-degree turn that would take her back into Russia and directly over the German base. Trudy started a slow descent and estimated how far she could glide from her now lower-than-three-thousand-foot altitude.

"If they don't hear me coming, I have a chance," Trudy said out loud.

Trudy could see the tower at the airfield and wondered if they had seen her and were attempting to call her over the radio. It seemed funny to her that this whole adventure had begun because of her dead stick landing at Mines Field, an experience that seemed years in the past after the recent traumatic events.

Trudy now judged that with a conservative glide path, she could make it to the runway with no power, and she turned off her engine. As Trudy dropped fast in a glide toward the field, she considered the possibility that her wreckage could block the runway and prevent her escape if the Mustang did not slide far enough after impact. As Trudy glided silently toward the enemy airfield, she decided to ignore past advice and lower the landing gear. As the landing gear under her wings fully extended, Trudy immediately felt the additional drag and instinctively pushed the stick a little bit farther forward to increase her rate of descent and also increase her airspeed to prevent a stall. With her engine off, Trudy would have no chance of recovering from a stall at her now six hundred feet of altitude above the field.

Trudy wanted to land near the middle of the airfield and slide to someplace near the end, but she was now descending too fast for that to happen, and she worried that she might have lowered the landing gear too soon and might not be able to reach the end of the runway.

As Trudy crossed the end of the runway a few seconds later, she pulled slightly back on the stick and performed an unconventional sharp flare only feet above the runway, stalling the plane and dumping it hard onto the runway.

Trudy applied the brakes and steered hard to the far side of the field, thinking that she might have more time there since the Germans would need to run the additional width of the runway when they inevitably tried to stop her.

Trudy noticed a lone Focke-Wulf FW-190 single-engine fighter and coasted the Mustang to the empty parking space next to it before she pushed hard on the brakes and the Mustang jerked to a stop.

Trudy was pleased to see that fuel was still flowing out of her right wing, fed by the higher fuselage tank with what was left of its additional eighty-five gallons of fuel.

As soon as she was stopped, Trudy noticed people running out of the hangar on the other side of the airfield, and she grabbed the survival pouch with the flare gun and exited her plane. Trudy made a mad dash to the FW-190 parked next to her. She clambered up into the fighter and started to try to make sense of the foreign instruments.

As the German soldiers running to greet her reached the edge of the runway, Trudy fired her first flare at the puddle of gasoline forming under the wing of her Mustang. She knew that she needed to destroy the Mustang, even if she didn't get away. Trudy aimed and fired the flare, which overshot the puddle of gasoline by several yards. Trudy frantically struggled to reload blindly while still attempting to figure out the German instrument panel.

Trudy attempted a second shot, which resulted in the Mustang erupt-ing into flames, and Trudy could feel the intense heat on her left side. The soldiers stopped running toward her when the fire erupted, but Trudy knew that they were still a threat, and now the burning Mustang would incinerate the German fighter with her in it if she did not move it. Trudy switched on something that looked like it must be the main power switch and then flipped on several other switches that looked like they might be for fuel pumps or carburetor heat.

Trudy pulled an ignition switch, and the propeller starting spinning, but the motor was not starting. She noticed what looked like a hand-pump primer and pushed that several times, feeling more resistance on the fourth push. She tried the starter again, and the propeller spun as it had before without starting. And then suddenly, with several puffs of white smoke, the motor started.

Trudy moved the throttle forward and taxied past the stunned Germans, who saw Trudy's long blond hair and were for a moment confused about what was going on. Trudy waved at the soldiers to increase their confusion, and a young soldier in the middle of the group waved back as the others wore looks that ranged from amusement to mild disbelief.

Trudy taxied to the end of the runway and noticed that the fuel gauge of the FW-190 seemed to show that it was full. At the end of the runway, Trudy spun the airplane around to face west and pushed the throttle forward to full power. The small fighter leaped forward, but it did not have nearly the acceleration that Trudy had become accustomed to in the Mustang. As Trudy passed her burning Mustang, she looked to the right across the field as fire trucks raced toward her burning plane.

Just past midfield, Trudy pulled back on the stick, and the FW-190 climbed away from the earth.

CHAPTER 23
Duxford, England,
22 1130 February 1944

"**S**ir, I am afraid we have some disturbing news," Captain Ryan said as he entered Colonel Campbell's office in the OSS operations building.

"Yes, come in, Captain Ryan. I assume that you are referring to our operation in Lithuania."

"Yes, sir, it is. We received a report through SOE channels that Major Jackson reportedly killed the senior SOE operative in Lithuania, who it turns out was also married to Professor Michalonis."

"Well, that it explains how they knew about the professor and his work in the first place. That doesn't explain why Major Jackson killed her, though," Colonel Campbell said as he reached for a bottle of Tennessee whiskey sitting on the table behind him and poured two glasses. "OK, Captain, I can see in your face there is more. Have a drink, and spill the beans. You know I don't like surprises from outside this HQ."

"Sir, SOE believes that Major Jackson was actually working for the NKVD and has taken the professor to Russia."

"Holy shit. All this time I suspected that he might be working for the SOE."

"Sir, our counterintelligence people think that he was working for SOE, but he may also have been recruited by the NKVD while he was in Spain, long before he ever went to England."

"OK, Rich, is there any news about Trudy?"

"Sir, we have one report via radio intercept that mentions an American fighter crashing and burning at a German fighter base just outside Kaunas.

There was reportedly a female pilot's body recovered from the badly burned wreckage of the aircraft."

"Goddamn it! Trudy was one of the best we had," Colonel Campbell yelled out.

"Sir, there may be one piece of good news here. A few minutes after we intercepted the report of the crash, there was another report that a female pilot had stolen an FW-190 from the same airfield."

"Outstanding! That has to be Trudy, unless the professor's wife could fly, too. When did that report come in?"

"Just about fifteen minutes ago, sir."

"OK, find out what kind of legs an FW-190 has, and report back how far she can go. I know those little German pieces of shit don't have the range of our Mustangs."

"Will do, sir. I did some initial checking before I came in, and it does look like Trudy should be able to make it to Denmark or Sweden."

"Good job, Captain. I hope she heads to Sweden. As you know, Sweden is neutral, and she will be interned until the end of the war if she lands there. If she lands someplace in Denmark, she has a good chance of getting caught by the Germans before she can contact the resistance and get back home."

"We have a very strong presence in Denmark, sir. Trudy knows that. I would bet that she heads there instead of sitting out the rest of the war in Sweden."

"Captain, I agree with you one hundred percent. Now get me details about how far Trudy can fly into Denmark from that airfield near Kaunas. Keep this close; do you understand?"

"Yes, sir," Captain Ryan said as he hurried out of Colonel Campbell's office.

Colonel Campbell picked up the phone. "Sandy, get me Colonel Nigel Scott over at SOE on the line. Tell him it's urgent and to ring me back," Colonel Campbell said as he slammed down the phone, stood up, and walked over to the map of northern Europe on his wall. He used a homemade calibrated measuring stick to check distances from the airfield and swept the measuring stick in an arc, trying to figure out where Trudy might end up if she was headed back to England. As the colonel stood and stared at the map, thinking, the phone rang.

"Colonel Campbell here."

"James, this is Nigel. I was told that you needed to speak to me on an urgent matter."

"Nigel, it looks like your boy Rod was working for the Russians, and the whole plan just blew up in our faces. Good news is we think that Miss Andrich has stolen an airplane from the Nazis and is trying to make her way back to England."

"James, that is the first good news I have heard today. She was, is, a wonderful young woman. What can I do to help you?"

"We have a radio intercept that someone stole an FW-190 from the airfield just east of Kaunas. That little piece of shit doesn't have the legs to get her back here, and we are trying to get an accurate estimate of how far she can get. We are guessing right now that it will be somewhere between four hundred and five hundred miles. I am guessing it will be closer to four hundred. Unless she is even better than I think she is, she won't know the cruising speed or the cruising altitude and will watch the fuel gauge and use a whole lot of Kentucky windage."

"I agree, four hundred miles is a good place to start. I am looking at a map now, and if she heads straight home, she will end up in Sweden or Denmark."

"Nigel, that is exactly what I figured, too, which is why I called. I need you to alert your SOE people in Denmark that we may soon have a pilot who needs help. I also want you to let your people in Sweden know."

"Sweden is neutral. We don't have anyone there, of course. I'm afraid that any American landing there will be interned for the duration of the war. Not much I can do about that, I'm afraid."

"Please let your people in Sweden know what is going on. I am asking for your help, not a confession."

"Very well, then, I can assure you that I will let everyone know who might be able to help her."

"Thank you, Nigel. One more quick thing. If your aircrew debriefings mention a lone FW-190, it would be good to know what happened."

"It would at that, James. Trust that I will keep you informed."

"Thank you, Nigel. Out, here," Colonel Campbell said as he hung up the phone and stared at the map contemplatively.

CHAPTER 24

The Baltic Sea, 22 1400 February 1944

Trudy was on a direct course for Denmark. She had no idea what the exact range of the FW-190 was but estimated it would be between four hundred and five hundred miles. Trudy knew that this direct flight path would take her over Sweden, but she decided to chance any encounters with the Swedes. Trudy had already heard that American pilots who performed emergency landings in Sweden were interned for the duration of the war, and Trudy knew that she had a lot more to contribute to the cause. Her number-one priority was to get to Denmark and link up with the Danish resistance.

Trudy also realized that she knew next to nothing about flying an FW-190, and if anything out of the ordinary occurred, she would not be able to recover from the emergency.

"Landing in Sweden is better than ditching in the Baltic Sea, freezing, and then drowning," Trudy said to herself.

Flying over water was boring on a good day, and this day could hardly be described as good. Trudy toyed with the fuel mixture and analyzed the gauges with the hope of figuring out the most efficient speed and fuel settings. Her concentration was suddenly interrupted by a pair of P-51B Mustangs and a stream of tracer rounds flowing past her canopy. It was at that moment that Trudy remembered that she was no longer wearing a parachute, after her rapid exit from her own Mustang in Kaunas.

Trudy slowed, waved her wings, and opened her canopy. She also pulled off her headgear and pulled her hair free to reveal her long blond hair, even though there was a slim chance that one of the Mustang pilots would get close enough to see her. As Trudy continued to wave her wings back and forth, the second Mustang made a gun run that damaged her oil cooler. Trudy watched the oil pressure drop and the engine temperature increase as the characteristic white smoke of burning oil flowed past the canopy.

Trudy knew that she would lose power soon and that without the lubricating and cooling oil, the engine would soon seize up in the best case and explode in the worst case.

The second P-51B noticed that Trudy was wagging her wings after he pulled the trigger, and he did end his run on the defenseless FW-190 early, or he would have certainly killed Trudy and destroyed the aircraft. The two Mustang pilots were almost certainly communicating with each other, and the first pilot unexpectedly flew alongside Trudy, staying just behind her wing, as he took a look. Satisfied that the FW-190 was not a threat to the bombers that he was sent to protect and also realizing that he was now in Swedish air space, both Mustangs waved their wings and headed southwest.

Trudy watched as the white smoke stopped and knew that her oil supply was gone. The engine stopped ten seconds later, and Trudy would now make her third dead-stick landing, only this time it would not be on an airfield.

Trudy was now at four thousand feet, and she could see a sandy coastline, curved like a lens just to her north. Not far inland were miles of cultivated fields. It was a cold day, and Trudy hoped that the ground would be frozen since she was going to attempt a landing with gear down.

As Trudy approached the coast, two biplanes with Swedish markings joined her and took up escort positions. Not knowing how to feather the propeller in the German plane and not even knowing whether it could be done, she found the propeller didn't turn at all and was producing a lot of drag, making the landing more difficult. One of the Swedish pilots immediately noticed that Trudy's propeller was not turning, and the Swedish planes no longer worried about being shot down by the superior German fighter. After communicating between themselves that the German plane would inevitably make a crash landing, the Swedish pilots quickly called their base and informed them that a German FW-190 was about to crash land in Swedish territory.

As the FW-190 approached the open fields, Trudy watched the altimeter and lowered the landing gear at six hundred feet, expecting that the fields were not much above sea level. Without a runway to line up with, Trudy lined up with the furrows in the field and attempted a three-point landing.

Trudy pulled back hard on the stick as she touched down, attempting to keep the tail down and the nose up, but with the lack of airspeed, the elevator provided very little down force, and Trudy nosed over, due to the resistance of the rich farmland soil. After the moderate impact, she caught her breath and exited the aircraft. The two biplanes each did a low pass, and then one of the biplanes orbited at about seven hundred feet while the other plane continued a series of low passes. Trudy raised her hands in the air for a moment during one of the plane's low passes and then sat down on a small dirt tractor trail with her feet in a dry ditch.

Trudy's head was nodding forward, and she was about to fall asleep when nearby police sirens woke her. Several police cars and military vehicles soon arrived. Soldiers and police rushed out, and two soldiers pushed her onto the ground and took away her shoulder holster and the M-1911. The two soldiers then reached under her shoulders and picked her up, half pulling and half lifting her toward a police car. A policeman was just about to help her into the car when Trudy pointed at her right leg and yelled out.

"Waffen. Fur Sie Bitte."

"Ach so, du bist Deutch."

"No, I am English," Trudy replied. "There is a weapon in my pants pocket. Take it."

The policeman patted down Trudy's leg and found the single-shot OSS throwaway .45 that Rich had given her. He looked shocked, and suddenly his tone changed.

"Where did you get this?" he demanded.

"I found it in the field here after I landed," Trudy lied.

"Tell me the truth, now," the policeman demanded.

"My name is Sonya Michalonis. Call the English Consulate in Malmo. They will know who I am," Trudy bluffed.

"There are no English in Malmo. Sweden is neutral. You will be interned. Your English is American. I have been there," the policeman said proudly.

"I teach English in Malmo to the employees of the British diplomats. I went to school in America."

"I don't believe you. Now turn around," the policeman said as he pushed her up against the side of the police car and handcuffed her.

"Say your name again," the policeman yelled.

"Sonya Michalonis," Trudy replied.

"That name is Lithuanian. You are a liar."

"Where are you taking me?" Trudy said with feigned fright.

"I am taking you to Ystad. Your status will be determined by the authorities there."

CHAPTER 25
Duxford, England,
24 0900 February 1944

"James, I think I have some very good news," Colonel Nigel Scott said after Colonel James Campbell answered the phone.

"What is it, Nigel? I saw a report that two of our Mustangs shot up an FW-190 and took credit for a kill two days ago. The pilot was alive, and they thought that the plane probably set down in Sweden. We are pretty sure that it was Trudy since one of the Mustang pilots reported that the pilot of the lone FW-190 was a woman with blond hair."

"Well, right, then. I believe that Miss Andrich has assumed the identity of Miss Sonya Michalonis. She apparently made an amazing landing in a farmer's field and walked away without a scratch."

"That doesn't surprise me one bit, Nigel."

"Well, the problem is she doesn't look a thing like Sonya, and it has the Swedes quite perplexed. They keep insisting to us that an American is pretending to be one of our staff in Malmo, and they want to know how the Americans would know so much about the British office in Malmo."

"Nigel, it's time for you to step up. You know what Miss Andrich is trying to pull off here, so just go with it. The Swedes don't even care as long as they have an explanation for their actions. You still have diplomatic relations with Sweden, so issue the young lady a replacement passport, and get her the hell back to England."

"James, I'm afraid it is not that simple. First, we need to explain to the Swedes why one of the British citizens who they generously allowed to enter their country is coming back from who knows where with a German fighter plane."

"Nigel, be creative. Tell them she was kidnapped, and if they push back, blame them for kidnapping her, and turn the tables on them."

"James, you know that I will do my best."

"Nigel, I know that you will. Thank you."

"All right, then, out, here, as you Americans are so fond of saying on the phone," Colonel Scott said as he hung up.

"Cheers, Nigel," Colonel Campbell said quietly into the disconnected phone before he hung up.

CHAPTER 26
Ystad, Sweden,
25 1300 February 1944

Trudy sat in the corner of a private, clean, and surprisingly roomy jail cell at the Ystad police headquarters. Two days of interrogation were very tiring, even if they never exceeded two hours without a break and there was no threat of physical abuse. When Trudy heard the jail-cell door unlock, she expected that since lunch was over, this would be another afternoon session of questions.

"Sonya, would you please come with me?" The detective who was the lead interrogator entered her cell with a female policewoman standing behind him.

Trudy got up and raised her hands in the air, knowing that the female policewoman would step forward, frisk her, and then handcuff her. Trudy felt the handcuffs go on once more and resisted her urge to turn and strangle her captor, knowing that would only make matters worse.

"Sonya, today a member of the Swedish Intelligence Service wishes to verify some of the details of your story. If you answer honestly, we might be able to make special arrangements for you. To that point, you might be able to leave here today. On the other hand, if you continue to lie to us, you will not even be granted internment status; you will continue to be treated as a criminal who entered our country in a stolen airplane while carrying illegal weapons."

"You do what you need to do. I already told you how I ended up in that airplane," Trudy said in monotone.

The detective led Trudy back to the interview room, as it was labeled. Trudy always called it the interrogation room, which always irritated the detective and his fellow "interviewers."

"Sonya, tell me again how you ended up in that German airplane?"

"It was a gift to make up for the fact that our sailing trip was a disaster and my boyfriend was embarrassed."

"And who was your boyfriend, once more?"

"He said that his name was Hermann and that he was in charge of the Luftwaffe," Trudy said in a deadpan voice.

"So you expect me to believe that you went sailing with Hermann Goering? That is preposterous!"

"Goering? Was that his name? He never told me his last name."

"Hermann Goering is the head of the Luftwaffe. You must know that?"

"No, but Hermann's sailing buddy, Mr. Speer, is really famous, I think."

"Mr. Speer? Albert Speer you mean? The head of all Nazi industry?"

"I never learned his first name. Is he really that important? If that was true, you would think that they could have obtained a better sailboat and, more importantly, a better compass."

"Do you see what I have been dealing with? All she will talk about is sailing with the most ridiculous sailing companions!" the detective yelled at the Swedish Intelligence Service Officer.

The intelligence officer grabbed the detective and pulled him out of the interview room, leaving Trudy by herself.

"You are an idiot, detective. Why didn't you call me sooner? The woman is either completely delusional or a highly trained intelligence officer. She has probably found it to be quite entertaining to screw with you for the past two days. Thank you for relieving her tedium. If I had had two days with her, I might have been able to figure out what was going on, but now with only thirty minutes before the Council General of the British delegation in Sweden arrives to pick her up, this is a total waste of time. I came all the way from Stockholm for this, you idiot!"

"Agent Stickhelm, this is my job, and I take it very seriously. This woman had weapons! She damaged a farmer's field with a stolen airplane. That is criminal behavior!" the detective yelled back.

"I am leaving now. You are an idiot, and now we will never know why this woman ended up in this situation and what the British are really up to here. Now, get out of my way," the intelligence officer said as he left the police headquarters in a huff.

As the intelligence officer stormed out of the police headquarters, a black Volvo sedan pulled up in front, and a skinny old man with a pipe and cane got out of the car and headed into the building.

After brief introductions and an exchange of handshakes with mid-level officials in the lobby, the chief of police hurried out of his office to meet the older man with the cane.

"Ambassador, what an honor to meet you. I understand that we have mistakenly detained one of your diplomats, and I want to offer my most sincere apologies."

"Thank you very much, but I am not the ambassador. Sir Sweetapple, minister of the Malmo legation, at your service. A pleasure, I am sure, Chief Tobako. There is a war going on, as we all understand, and one can't be too careful under these circumstances."

"Sir, Miss Michalonis is in the interview room. You can meet her there, and then we can get some proper clothing for her. Please come with me, sir."

The fat, pompous police chief led Sir Sweetapple back to the interrogation room.

"Interview room? Well, isn't that a clever name for it, chief," Sir Sweetapple commented sarcastically.

The chief led the way into the room. Trudy remained seated, expecting some sort of act of trickery to get her to change her story.

"Sonya, it is so good to see you. I love what you have done with your hair! There was perhaps a little bit more red in it before all of your recent sea adventures in salt spray and sun. Colonel Scott and Colonel Campbell both send their regards."

Trudy's eyes reacted to the mention of Colonel Scott and Colonel Campbell, and she worried for a moment that she had given away her identity to a clever Swedish interrogator.

"It is so good to see you, sir," Trudy said with a very enthusiastic tone.

"Sonya, I am pleased to provide you with your replacement diplomatic passport and letter of introduction from His Majesty. Please be more careful with these documents in the future," Sir Sweetapple said as he placed the documents in Trudy's hand for her to examine.

"I will make arrangements for Miss Michalonis to get cleaned up, and we will get some proper clothing for her," the detective offered.

"Oh nonsense, chief. I'm afraid that we don't have time for that now. Sonya can wear my coat until we get back to Malmo," Sir Sweetapple said as he removed his black wool greatcoat and wrapped it around Trudy's shoulders. "Come, dear, there are a lot of people who can't wait to see you back safe and sound."

Sir Sweetapple led Trudy directly to his car. He held the door for her while she got in and then jumped in beside her and motioned for his driver to drive.

"Well played, Trudy. We will get you out of here and back to America in no time. And, no doubt, to a hero's welcome."

"I am afraid that you have me confused with someone else. My name is Sonya," Trudy said as she stuck to her cover story.

"Dear, I understand what you are doing, and I can't say that I blame you, so for now, Sonya it is."

CHAPTER 27
Duxford, England, 01 1130 March 1944

"**W**elcome back, Trudy. General Donovan sends his regards and congratulations. Even though it may take a decade to replicate Mikhalonis's research, it was the right move on your part to take him out. Instead of curing illness as the professor intended, the Russians could have used his knowledge to develop biological weapons that target specific races or ethnicities. If the next war is against them, this might make all the difference," Colonel Campbell said.

"Thank you, sir. I can't tell you how disconnected I feel. It is almost like the safety here in England is some kind of a dream or illusion. It was so different over there."

"I understand. It will take some time to get used to things again. No one is trying to kill you here, and your toughest challenge will be the traffic or a boss who happens to get up on the wrong side of the bed once in a while. That's the perspective that you will develop after time brings distance from the horrible things you saw and maybe even had to do. After time allows you that perspective, everything else becomes easy."

"I can see that. I'm definitely not there yet. But what about when we need to do it again or even over and over?"

"Then we heal once more and treasure those we love. So many have had to deal with much more than this. I understand that there was a young pilot who mourned your loss and flew countless hours in the hope of finding you. If I were you, I would pick up where you left off. If you need to do this again, I am sure that he will be your anchor."

"Gus searched for days? We were only going out on our first date the night I disappeared."

"He flew as many hours as Colonel Straight would allow. Colonel Straight picked him up as a test pilot for the factory team after he got to know him from that experience."

"I'm dead. How can I go back now?" Trudy asked with tears starting to form in the corners of her eyes.

"We have a rather adventurous plan in the works that will give you a bit of time to relax before you get back into the daily flying routine again. I'll fill you in on the exact details tomorrow. In the meantime, I think that Captain Ryan would like a word with you. I am stepping out for a few minutes for coffee, so feel free to use my office."

Captain Ryan entered the colonel's office. As soon as Colonel Campbell pulled the door closed behind him, Rich rushed forward to welcome Trudy with a hug.

"I honestly didn't expect to see you again," Rich said as he held Trudy close.

"The last time I saw you, an MP had just hit you over the head. I think I was rude for a moment, too. Whatever happened about that?"

"I don't remember you being rude. Either you weren't, or the blow to the head erased it. I did try to make an issue of it and get those MPs busted down, but the colonel convinced me that I kind of deserved it, so I let it go."

"I'm glad you're all right. I owe you some sincere thanks. I might not be standing here if you had not provisioned me with that knife. Unfortunately, the Swedes took it away," Trudy answered.

Rich stepped back and looked Trudy up and down.

"You look the same, but I know you don't feel the same inside. If you need to talk, I have been through this, too."

"Thank you, Rich. I might just take you up on that. Maybe after a few drinks sometime soon."

"That would need to be tonight, then, because my job is to get you back into the WASP mainstream without too many questions. Take a seat, and I'll fill you in on the plan."

Trudy sat down on the colonel's couch, and Rich sat down on a comfortable chair across a low coffee table from Trudy.

"Most of the world thinks that you are dead due to a midair collision with Major Jackson off the coast of California. We need to bring you back to life with a credible story. Rod is dead, and the crash explains that without admitting what a traitor he was. That will no doubt save his family a lot of embarrassment and pain. You, on the other hand, drifted for a week in your life raft and were picked up by a Mexican commercial fishing vessel headed out for a month-long excursion to the Galapagos. You will need to study up on the Galapagos."

"Yeah, me and Darwin. I always admired him anyhow."

"After the Mexican boat filled its hold with fish, it docked back in Tijuana. You will be expected to contact Colonel Straight at Mines Field after we drop you off in Tijuana, and they will send someone to pick you up. You can call him the day you arrive. You can call him after a week in the sun, or you can call him never. It's your choice since officially you are dead until you make that call."

"I don't think that my death will last long since I don't have a penny to my name at this point," Trudy said with a frown.

"Well, that is not entirely true. We owe you quite a bit of back pay, danger pay, and per diem, so please accept this envelope for any expenses. I do need you to sign this receipt, though."

Trudy looked in the envelope, and there were literally thousands of dollars in hundred-dollar bills. She signed the receipt without even reading the amount.

"Thank you. One more thing—your friend Gus is permanently stationed at Mines Field now as the senior flight instructor and test pilot. Here is his phone number and Colonel Straight's number, too, courtesy of Colonel Campbell," Rich said with a very sad tone.

"Thank you, Rich. That is so kind of both of you."

"Trudy, here is the bad news. Right now your flight records end at a midair collision with Rod. There will be a board of inquiry. Rod turned into you in the fog without warning. Period. You were able to parachute out of your damaged plane, and Rod tried to recover his damaged aircraft and hit the water at high speed. No extra details, just stick to that short story."

"I understand."

"Also, since you have not flown for almost two months according to your official flight records, you will need to perform flight refresher training, so you may want to keep Gus's number handy."

"I wonder if Gus can fly a trainer airplane into Tijuana," Trudy said with a beaming smile. "We might just make a really good team."

CPSIA information can be obtained
at www.ICGtesting.com
Printed in the USA
LVOW07s1709110417
530416LV00002B/496/P